*Prince Henry
the Navigator*

Also by
Thomas Caldecot Chubb
The Venetians: Merchant Princes

Prince Henry the Navigator

and the Highways of the Sea

THOMAS CALDECOT CHUBB

The Viking Press

New York

To Percy Chubb II,

who has sailed some

of Henry's seas

Cover painting by Richard M. Powers
Chapter head drawings and map on page 6 by Laurel Brown

First published in 1970 by The Viking Press, Inc.
625 Madison Avenue, New York, N.Y. 10022
Published simultaneously in Canada by
The Macmillan Company of Canada Limited
Printed in U.S.A.

Library of Congress catalog card number: 78–106923
623.899   1. History of Navigation
B   1. Henry the Navigator

VLB 670–57624–7   670–57623–9
2   3   4   5   74   73   72

Contents

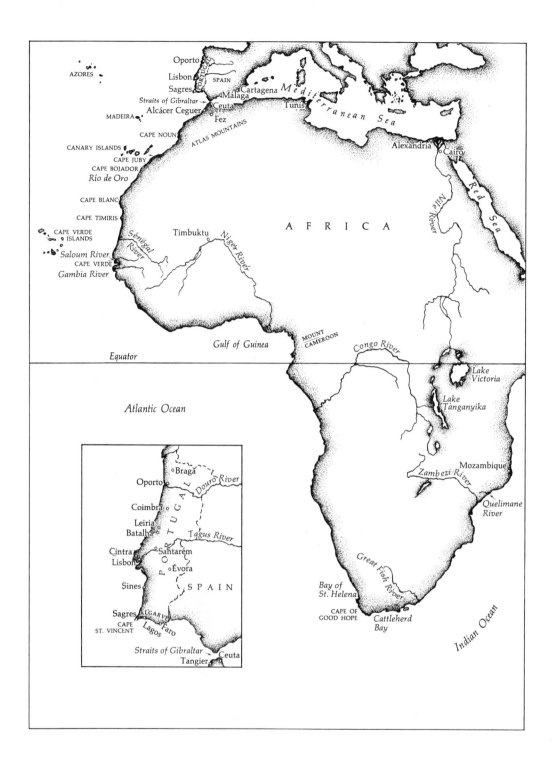

Oporto
Lisbon
Sagres
Straits of Gibraltar
Alcácer Ceguer
AZORES
MADEIRA
CAPE NOUN
CANARY ISLANDS
CAPE JUBY
CAPE BOJADOR
Río de Oro
CAPE BLANC
CAPE TIMIRIS
CAPE VERDE ISLANDS
Saloum River
CAPE VERDE
Gambia River

PORTUGAL
SPAIN
Cartagena
Málaga
Ceuta
Fez
ATLAS MOUNTAINS
Tunis

Mediterranean Sea

Alexandria
Cairo
Red Sea
Nile River

A F R I C A

Sénégal River
Timbuktu
Niger River

Gulf of Guinea
MOUNT CAMEROON

Congo River

Lake Victoria
Lake Tanganyika

Equator

Atlantic Ocean

Mozambique
Zambezi River
Quelimane River

Braga
Oporto
Coimbra
Leiria
Batalha
Cintra
Lisbon
Santarém
Évora
Sines
Sagres
CAPE ST. VINCENT
Lagos
Faro
Straits of Gibraltar
Tangier
Ceuta

PORTUGAL
SPAIN
ALGARVE
Douro River
Tagus River

Bay of St. Helena
CAPE OF GOOD HOPE
Cattleherd Bay
Great Fish River

Indian Ocean

The
Spices
and Splendors
of the East

On the ninth day of September, 1499, all of Portugal scorched under a blazing sun. It also slumbered. In the countryside the vines were heavy, but as noon neared there were few peasants who would venture forth to carry the purple grapes to the wine presses, where bare feet would trample out their tangy juices. The grain fields were beginning to turn golden, but it was too hot for the farmers, men and women, to swing their gleaming sickles. Goat bells hardly tinkled. The scraggly herds and the flocks of merino sheep found it more pleasant to recline in the shadows of olive trees or cork oaks than to graze on the sparse grass of parched brown pastures. The sun-blackened boys who herded them found the shade more pleasant too. Even at sea, and off half a hundred golden beaches, the high-prowed fishing craft (they were much like the vessels which had been introduced by the Phoenicians a thousand or more years earlier) rolled lazily on an ocean whose swells seemed to be made of glass.

The towns and the cities were just as somnolent. In the

markets one did not hear the customary sad, quavering cries of the vendors, nor did oxen, flowers twined around their horns, lumber through the streets beside the gray pannier-laden donkeys. The people who might have driven them were, very wisely, indoors.

Except in one place. The little port of Restello—it is now called Belém (Bethlehem), and has become a suburb of Lisbon—teemed with activity. Its streets and beaches were crowded with people: fishermen, even in those days wearing the traditional black stocking-cap; full-skirted and raucous-voiced *varinas* (fishwives); *lavradores* (field workers) from the farms; shopkeepers and merchants from their nearby places of business; and caulkers, carpenters, and riggers from the shipyards. Even here and there a *fidalgo* (nobleman) clad in brightly colored silk or satin and wearing a sword at his side.

All of them looked toward the west. Before long they saw what they had come to see. A faint blur on the horizon loomed larger and larger until it became the three sails of a lateen-rigged vessel that bounded gaily toward them over the sheltered waters of the Tagus River (the "River of Straw," on whose banks Lisbon stands—called this because although its waters were sometimes leaden, more often they sparkled as if strewn with a thousand golden straws). It was the long-awaited caravel from Terceira in the Azores, and on board was a rough, square-shouldered, spade-bearded seaman. He was not more than forty years old, yet he looked as rugged and as weather-beaten as the sea god Neptune.

Vasco da Gama he was, son of the *alcaide* (military governor) of Sines, a fishermen's port in southwest Portugal. A little over two years ago (July 8, 1497), he had set sail from this very spot as *capitão mor* (captain major, or admiral) of a fleet of four vessels. Two of them were *naus*, large three-masted vessels weighing perhaps two hundred tons each. These were his flagship, the *São Gabriel*, and her sister ship, the *São Raphael*. The third vessel was a caravel, the *Berrios*, and the last a clumsy supply ship.

His orders had been "to make discoveries and find spices." Now he had come back again, with only two of his vessels and fifty-five of the hundred and seventy men he had set out with. (Tropical diseases and scurvy had decimated the crews, and Vasco had destroyed the *São Gabriel* and the supply ship because he did not have enough sailors to man them.) If one could believe the tales told by the *Berrios* men and the *São Raphael* men—Vasco had sent these two vessels ahead of him while he took his dying brother to the Azores—he had accomplished his mission and more than that.

Vasco's "land of spices" was India, and he had boasted that he would sail there. Now he had done so. Twenty thousand miles he had sailed! That was the length of his round trip—almost the distance around the world. It was a voyage such as no one had ever made before.

Yet the idea of making it did not originate in Vasco's own mind. The fact that he wanted to sail from Portugal to India, and even more important, the fact that he *could* sail there, was in large part the result of the labors and studies of a man who was no longer living; a man who had in fact died in the very year in which Vasco da Gama was born.

To his Portuguese countrymen he was O Infante Dom Henrique (the king's son, Lord Henry); he was also the Duke of Viseu and the Grand Master of the Order of Christ. But although he never commanded a ship and only stood upon the deck of one on the three occasions when he was a captain of soldiers, he has gone down in history as Prince Henry the Navigator. It is a good name, for even though Henry did not navigate the oceans himself, he taught other men how to. He made navigation a science, and having done so, he sent out his captains and his explorers in all directions, but mainly down the coast of West Africa. He told them that some day they would come to the end of that continent and that then they would round it.

Without Henry's pioneering work Vasco would never have been able to sail to India, nor would he have been given the reception that awaited him at Restello. And what a reception it was!

On that scorching September day, Vasco's vessel neared the end of her journey. Over the bar she went, her bow dashing aside white spray, and then as she neared the strand she rounded into the wind. Down came yards and sails, and the anchor splashed into the water. She swung idly as eager hands lifted the batel (the ship's boat) from its berth amidships and eased it overboard. Vasco took his place in its stern, and pine oars lashed the water. Minutes later—to applause that reverberated—he stepped upon his native shore.

Nine days later Vasco was applauded once again, this time by the man who had sent him on his voyage.

Dom Manoel I, thirty years old, fair of hair and complexion, thin, hard-working, moderate in what he ate and drank, even if somewhat vain and exceedingly fond of pomp and display, has gone down in history as King Emanuel the Fortunate. This is because he was a very lucky man. Not only did he mount the throne almost by accident—his cousin, Prince Affonso, who should have succeeded João II, was killed by a fall from his horse, and Manoel's own elder brother had been murdered—but nearly all his great wealth and glory came to him from the work of others.

On that September day Dom Manoel watched Vasco's arrival from a royal palace of his which was perched upon a hill at Cintra, but he did not immediately mount a steed and ride with a retinue to greet his captain major. Instead he allowed Vasco time to settle his affairs, mourn his brother, and pray once again at the square, simple little chapel where he and his crewmen had prayed the night before they set sail. (To commemorate Vasco's voyage, Manoel would later replace this chapel with the ornate and magnificent monastery of the Hieronymites. It is one of the most beautiful edifices in Portugal.)

Not until September 18 did Manoel descend to the shore, sending ahead of him his command that Vasco should have a triumphant entry into Lisbon. And indeed Vasco did! Bagpipes whined, trumpets blared, drums boomed, and cannons thundered as noblemen and great citizens, led by their king, conducted the seaman through winding, banner-draped streets from the shore of Restello to the Lisbon *sé*, or cathedral. There solemn mass was celebrated.

Then Manoel led the captain major to his nearby Limoeiro (Lemon Tree) Palace and seated him in a private chamber.

"Tell me your story," he commanded. Vasco obeyed.

In the beginning, to be sure, it was not much of a tale. By 1497 the sea road from Lisbon to the Canaries was a well-traveled route. Sailing it was little more adventurous than sailing down the Tagus, and even when Vasco's fleet was separated by fog off Terra Alta (now Spanish West Africa) the waters were still well-known enough for its vessels to rejoin each other in a sandy bay at São Tiago, the southernmost of the Cape Verde Islands. There—"joyfully," according to the captain major—they stayed a week, taking on goat meat and fresh water.

But then the troubles began.

"My fleet left São Tiago on August 3," said Vasco, "and for two weeks and two hundred leagues we were baffled by calm after calm, followed by baffling winds which blew from every direction, and then by violent squalls which brought zigzag-ging lightning that split the heavens, and by torrential rains." (We know now that this was typical doldrum weather, es-pecially for June, July, and August, and that Vasco and his vessels had reached the doldrums—the waters near the equator.)

Finally a squall more savage than the rest struck the fleet, and in the middle of a pitch-black night a loud crack was heard aboard the *São Gabriel;* as the ship rolled and pitched, ropes and canvas came down in a wild tangle of confusion. Immediately Vasco sent a man aloft. When he came down again, he reported that the main yard was sprung. If nothing was done, it would soon carry away.

"So I had no choice but to lay for two days and a night under foresail, and lower main while repairs were made. During this time I determined to change my course. Instead of sailing due southeast for the tip of Africa, I would sail west for a while and after that, make my southing. Only then would I again head toward my destination. It was my one chance of finding winds that would take me where I wanted to go."

This he did. The spar was sprung on August 18, and on August 20 Vasco headed his vessels southwest, crossing the equator with the breeze just forward of amidships on the port side, and continuing in this direction until he had reached latitude 10° south. (At his westernmost point, incidentally, Vasco had come within six hundred miles of the coast of Brazil!)

Then he changed his course a second time—to southeast, east, and finally, still seeking the Cape of Good Hope, east by north.

"Your Majesty, for ninety-five days we were alone on the wild and empty ocean, and not until October 22 did we even have a hint of anything but mile after unending mile of water.

But on that day, toward dusk, we saw flocks of birds that resembled herons. As our ships approached, they flew off in a south southeasterly direction as if they were going toward land."

These may have been *gaivotas*, large gulls with dark wings and white bodies which are sometimes found over the south Atlantic Ocean. They were undoubtedly flying toward the island of Tristão da Cunha, four hundred miles distant.

The ships were now in the fresh and lively westerlies and were also helped along by an eastward flowing current. They literally began to leap forward. Their average daily run was 131 miles.

"On October 27," Vasco continued, "we saw many whales and also *quoquas* [perhaps sea lions] and seals." Pigfish (porpoises) and dorados (dolphins) were also sighted.

On November 1 they spotted quantities of gulfweed. This indicated they were nearing the coast. Then on November 4 at nine o'clock in the morning they sighted land. At this, there was a celebration. The men put on their gala clothes, the yards were dressed with flags and banners, and there was a roar that shook the welkin as Vasco was saluted as captain major by every bombard in the fleet.

However they did not drop anchor, for not even Vasco's pilot, Pero d'Alenquer, who had been with Bartholomeu Dias when he rounded the Cape of Good Hope, recognized the place. Instead, after tacking back and forth for a while, they stood out to sea again.

"On November 7," said Vasco, "we approached the land once more and found a broad and well-sheltered bay with good holding ground. We named it the Bay of St. Helena."

Although they still had not reached the Cape, that was the moment when the Portuguese really should have fired their bombards. Vasco and his men had now traveled at least seven thousand miles, and of these, more than five thousand were over wide stretches of open ocean that no ship had sailed before (Dias had largely clung to the shore line). This was, at the time, the longest and possibly the most difficult feat of deep-sea sailing ever accomplished.

But Vasco's never-ending difficulties were not over. These, he told his king, grew greater.

To begin with, he still had the Cape of Good Hope to round. Dias had named it Cape Stormy and it lived up to this name. As Vasco approached it wild gales began to blow and so furious were they that, according to one of his sailors, they drove his vessels far enough south for him to see ice floes. Only then did they subside, allowing him to turn back toward land.

With the Cape rounded, Vasco worked eastward from Dias's Cattleherd Bay (today it is Mossel Bay) toward Great Fish River (near modern Port Alfred), which was the farthest point reached by Dias. On the way he had to contend with head winds and adverse currents which were so baffling that upon one occasion the Portuguese were driven out to sea and then crawled back again, only to find themselves at the same Ilhéo da Cruz (Cross Island) they had left five days before. When at last they turned north, it was necessary to sail through narrow, often mangrove-choked channels that wound their way between the shore and the outlying islands and shoals. The *São Raphael* grounded on one of those shoals with a great crash at least six miles off the mainland. The Portuguese set out anchors and warps, but despite all they could do, she lay high and dry until the next flood tide.

There were two or three thousand miles of these channels and shoals, and not one of them had been charted!

In addition to these problems, Vasco had to deal with—to learn *how* to deal with—the people he encountered, and with their rulers. To be sure, his first encounter had a comic aspect. Vasco laughed as he told about it.

"We stayed at the Bay of St. Helena for eight days," he said, "to careen and clean our ships—to scrape off the barnacles and repair our sails—and also to observe the latitude more accurately than we could from the deck of a ship." (He found it to be 32° 30' south. Actually it is 32° 40' south. He made an error of a little less than seven miles!)

"While we were there we made friends with the tawny-colored, skin-clad, cattle-raising inhabitants." These were Hottentot tribesmen. "We took one of them captive, fed him, clad him in our Portuguese clothing, and then sent him ashore. After that they came in groups of fifty or sixty and were quite eager to trade metal-plated shells and foxtail fans for *çeitils* [a copper Portuguese coin, worth about one quarter of a cent], little round bells, or rings made of tin."

One of Vasco's soldiers, Fernão Velloso, asked for permission to go ashore with the visitors "to see how they lived and what they ate." Permission was granted and off he went. Shortly afterward his escorts caught a seal, and when they came to a nearby hill, they roasted it and gave him some. Then Fernão suddenly turned back and came running toward the ship, staggering and stumbling in the heavy sand. A crowd, hurling stones and throwing assagais (slender wooden javelins), pursued him.

"Rescue!" he shouted. "Rescue! Rescue!"

He was dragged into the Portuguese boat and there he insisted that he had been well-treated by the tribesmen.

"Then why," asked a sailor, "did you come down the hill so much faster than you went up it?"

"I knew," said Fernão, undaunted, "that sooner or later they would attack us, and how could you hold them off without my help?" (The truth, it turned out, was that when Fernão had asked to be taken to the Hottentots' kraal, they had turned on him.)

Two hundred Hottentots of the same tribe awaited Vasco

and his men after they had rounded the Cape, and although at first they tried to keep the Portuguese from landing, they were soon trading with them. They even sold Vasco a black ox, "whose meat," he said, "was as tasty as the beef of Portugal." After that, to the sound of goras (native instruments), they regaled him with a tribal dance.

Even as far north as the Rio do Cobre (now the Inharrime in Mozambique) Vasco was greeted in a friendly manner by a tall, handsome people who were still far enough away from European civilization to be impressed by men wearing suits of iron (armor) and sailing in such enormous vessels. *Almadias* —this was how the Portuguese pronounced the native *el maziyah*, or ferryboat—was the word used. It means dugout canoes.

Their chief was even taller than his followers, and to him Vasco's interpreter, Martin Affonso, presented a jacket, a pair of red pantaloons, a fez, and some bracelets. These the chief put on at once. Then he led Martin to his dwelling to reward him with a feast of millet porridge and fowl, and to let his subjects gawk at this strange being.

"Look what I have been given! Look what I have been given!" he shouted as he danced in front of Martin. His subjects clapped their hands.

Two weeks later, however, the Portuguese were not greeted with either awe or delight. They had now come to the Quelimane River—it seems to have been just north of the Zambezi, and flowed through a "low coast thickly wooded with tall trees"—and two or three days after they had anchored off its swampy mouth, they were visited by two local noblemen (Vasco called them *senhores*), who spat scornfully at the gifts the Portuguese offered them.

"We do not value the trash you want to give us," said one of them, using signs to make his meaning clear and shaking his silk-fringed *touca* (cap).

"Nor are we impressed by your ships," added the other, using signs too. He was wearing a green satin turban. "We have with us a young man who has seen ships as big or bigger."

"Our hearts rejoiced at this, Your Majesty," said Vasco, "for it appeared that we were nearing the goal of our desires, namely India. And we therefore named the river the Rio dos Bons Signaẽs (River of Good Omens)."

Vasco also doubled his vigilance, for if there were such ships they were Arab ships. The Arabs—and the shrewd Swahili-speaking Africans who joined them in their profitable trade ventures—were Moslems. In those days Moslems and Christians were sworn enemies, and on the sails of Vasco's vessels the red cross of the Order of Christ was displayed flamboyantly. From now on the Portuguese could look for every kind of trickery, treachery, or show of force.

It was well that they did, for at Mozambique (Monconbiquy to Vasco) and later at Mombasa—the latter has become a thriving seaport whose freighters carry every kind of local product from kapok to aluminum ware all over the world—they encountered all three. In Vasco's time Mozambique and Mombasa were small towns with many mosques and minarets. Both were located on small coral islands close to the mainland. In their bazaars and along their water fronts red Moors (the natives) had traded from time immemorial with white Moors (the Arabs of Arabia) in everything from foodstuffs to precious stones. Each town was ruled by a sheik, or royal governor, who called himself a sultan. Both sheiks were, as they had to be, very crafty men.

The sheik who ruled Mozambique was named Zacoeja, and he received the Portuguese with seeming friendship. He even gave them some welcome news.

"Yea," he said through a Moorish interpreter, "there are many Christians nearby. Indeed there is a wealthy island, half

Moorish and half Christian. Yea, the realm of Prester John is near too." Prester John (John the Priest) was a legendary Christian monarch who was thought to dwell in either the Indies or Africa. Vasco had been instructed to try to find him as well as spices.

To maintain Zacoeja's good will Vasco gave him hats, *marlotas* (rough cloaks), and coral, but he received these scornfully and demanded scarlet cloth instead. "Despite this, he gave us in return native produce of all kinds, including a fruit as large as a melon, of which only the rind is eaten." This was a coconut.

Sultan Zacoeja also offered the Portuguese two pilots.

Men who knew the coast! Vasco accepted their services with alacrity, and one of them promptly lured him to an island where four or five boats filled with armed men—they carried "bows and long arrows" and were protected by bucklers— appeared and attacked the Portuguese. Vasco drove them off but could not sink them.

Between Mozambique and Mombasa, the Portuguese were attacked at least once more, but this time, they were forewarned by one of Zacoeja's pilots. He had been rudely flogged for his treachery and this unsealed his lips. Instead of being captured when they went ashore to fill their water kegs, Vasco and his men drove off a band of twenty or more howling warriors armed with assagais, poniards, bows, and slings. Then, with bombards mounted on their boats, they battered down the palisaded village from which the warriors had come, and captured three of their fleeing dugouts, which were laden with cotton stuffs, palm-frond baskets, glazed jars filled with butter, glass vials of scented water, and "some books of their law"—i.e. the Koran.

At Mombasa, several hundred miles farther north, it was the same. Said Vasco: "We anchored off Mombasa on April

7 and at midnight were approached by a *zavra* (a native dhow) carrying one hundred men. They came to my flagship and wanted to come aboard, but I permitted only four or five at a time. I think that they had come as spies."

The next day the captain major was welcomed officially.

"The Sultan sent me a sheep and large quantities of oranges, lemons, and sugar cane, as well as a ring which was supposed to be a guarantee of safety. These were brought to me by two men who were almost white and who said that they were Christians. In return I sent him a string of coral beads; but two days later when both our pilots jumped overboard, I became suspicious, and made two Moors, whom I had seized earlier, speak up by dropping boiling oil upon them. They said orders had been given to capture us as we lay at anchor, and surely enough, about midnight, two dugouts crowded with men appeared. Those aboard them jumped into the water and swam toward the *Berrios* and the *São Raphael*. They had planned to cut our cables and set us adrift. We first thought they were a school of tuna—we could hear them splashing and our mouths watered—but we soon discovered our error and shouted to the other vessels. Although the natives had already gotten hold of the rigging of the mizzen masts, they were driven off."

Indeed, it was not until they reached the city of Malindi (near the equator in modern Kenya, two thirds of the way up the east coast of Africa) that the Portuguese finally fared better.

"This Malindi," Vasco told his king, "lies in a deep bay and it extends for many miles along the shore. Its houses are lofty and whitewashed and they have many windows. It is surrounded by groves of palm trees and by fields of grain and vegetables. In fact," he concluded tactfully—but after desert and veld and jungle, it must have seemed true to him—

"it is like Alcochete on the river Tagus where Your Majesty was born."

But Malindi had more to offer Vasco and his men than reminders of home.

"We found here four vessels belonging to Christian Indians," Vasco said. This was a mistake Vasco and his men were to make often. They thought they had heard those on the four vessels shouting "Christ! Christ!" but in fact they were shouting "Krishna!" Krishna is the second person of the Hindu trinity.

But at least they were Indians. With their dusky skins, scant clothing, and refusal to eat beef, there was no doubt about it. Vasco rejoiced. For if they could sail *from* India, he could sail *to* India. And soon he had the means to do so.

Wajeraj—he was not the sultan or even sheik of Malindi, but merely regent for his ailing father—had been well informed about the four Portuguese ships with their blazing artillery, and he did not wish to incur their anger.

But why merely avoid their anger? Why not win their friendship? If he could make their commander his ally, he could free himself from the overlordship of the Sultan of Kilwa, who was master of Malindi and the other cities and towns along the coast. He could perhaps become the overlord himself.

"Forthwith," said Vasco, "Wajeraj set out to gain my good will. He invited me to come to his palace to rest, and when I told him that Your Majesty had forbidden me to land until I reached India"—he had, of course, landed before, but this was a convenient excuse—"he had himself rowed to the *São Gabriel* in a royal barge.

"It was a scene that dazzled the eyes," the captain major continued. "The monarch was clad in a damask robe trimmed with green satin. He wore a magnificent turban and was seated on a cushioned bronze chair. Over his head was held a crimson parasol, and beside him stood an ancient attendant, who carried a short sword in a silver sheath. Another boat, manned by slaves, brought six sheep and sacks of cloves, cumin, nutmeg, ginger, and pepper. 'These are for your king,' I was told. I was also promised nine days of fetes, sham battles, and music played on *anafils* and other copper and ivory trumpets.

" 'I only want a pilot who will guide me to the land these spices come from,' I replied.

" 'And I only the help of the great king, your master.'

" 'When I return,' I said.

"A week later he complied with my request. He sent me a Christian pilot named Malema Canaqua." (Actually he was a Moslem from the Gujerat in western India, and "Mallim Kanaka" was a title meaning sailing master. His real name was Ibn Hajid.)

"We were much pleased with him, Your Majesty. We found that he was as familiar as we were with the Genoese needle"— the magnetic compass, called this because it was introduced into Portugal by Genoese shipmen—"and that he understood the use of quadrants·and that his navigating charts and portolanos (sailing directions) were as good as any in the world."

With high hopes and Ibn Hajid to guide them, Vasco and his companions set sail again on April 24. For two days, they skirted the African coast, heading toward "a huge bay and a strait"—the Red Sea and scorching Bab el Mandeb—"in which were large cities and six hundred known islands."

Then, "favored by the winds," they "headed across the open sea. On April 29, we saw the North Star again." They had finally recrossed the equator! "On Friday, May 19, after having seen no land for twenty-three days, we sighted a lofty mountain, and having sailed before the wind the whole time, we could not have made less than six hundred leagues."

He underestimated. A league is approximately three miles, and it is 2500 miles from Malindi to Mount Ely in the Western Ghats of India.

"We soon reached the coast, but before we could find a place to anchor, we were driven off shore by torrential rains and a violent thunderstorm. This was on May 19, and there was nothing we could do except beat back and forth, drenched to the skin, and hope for a break in the weather. It came the next day. On May 20, the clouds lifted and we could see mountains again. And Ibn Hajid now knew where we were. He said that we were just above Calicut and directed us to sail toward it. At nightfall, we anchored two leagues from the city. Your Majesty, I was trembling in every limb. I knelt upon the deck and lifted my hands to heaven as I gave my thanks to God."

Vasco and his men stayed at Calicut or at the nearby and safer port of Pandanari for a little more than three months, and well they might have. It held almost everything they sought.

Even today Calicut—now known as Kozhikode—is one of the busiest cities in southwest India. In Vasco's time, it was much more than that. Writing in 1349, the great Arab traveler, Ibn Battuta, said that only Alexandria, Quilon (farther south in India), Soldaia (a Genoese port in the Crimea), and Zayton (Amoy in China) were equal to it in magnificence and trade. This was still true in 1498. When Vasco dropped anchor here he found 1500 vessels, dhows and junks among them, crowding the harbor. They came from Africa, Egypt, Arabia, the Persian Gulf, Malacca, Sumatra, Siam, Indochina, and even China and Japan. And they carried every kind of cargo.

The pungent spices Vasco came to seek of course abounded: cinnamon ("both the leaves and boughs of the same"), pepper, ginger, frankincense, civet musk, ambergris, and storax. But the marts also sold lac and brazilwood, and nearby was an island (Zilon, or Ceylon) where one could buy ivory and elephants. For years Calicut itself had woven a cloth much like present-day madras, and there was an abundance of satins, taffetas, gold brocades and scarlet. Pearls were plentiful too—and cheap—and excellent sapphires and balass rubies were offered by the trayful.

Moreover, since in payment the merchants took only gold and silver—or in rare cases, coral, copper kettles, wine, oil, tartar, and spectacles ("for," as Vasco noted, "there are countries where a pair of these fetches a high price")—gold and silver were everywhere. Even Venetian and Genoese ducats circulated, although gold xerafins coined by the Sultan of Babylonia (Egypt) were more in evidence. Indeed, so plentiful were these precious metals that even the poor people used them in their ornaments. The men, said Vasco, "pierce their ears and wear much gold in them." As for the women, who "as a rule are ugly and of small stature, they wear many jewels of gold around the neck, numerous bracelets on their arms, and rings set with precious stones on their toes."

Vasco, with as much tact as was available to one of his rough-and-ready nature, attempted to establish friendly relations with the man who controlled all this splendor and who could hold it back or make it accessible as he saw fit.

In the beginning, the captain major was successful. The ruler of Calicut was the zamorin—this was the Portuguese rendition of "Samudryah Rajah," or King of the Seacoast—and the zamorin sent his kotwal (military governor) to Vasco.

"His Majesty has commanded me to invite you to his palace—you and thirteen of your men," he said.

"I accept gladly," the captain major replied.

Ashore they went, clad in their best attire. They were conducted—Vasco in a palanquin borne by six men—to the house of a principal citizen. There they were provided with a dinner "which consisted," Vasco said, "of rice with much butter"—probably clarified butter, or ghee—"and excellent fish." Then along a road "crowded with a countless multitude"—including women with babes in their arms—"who were anxious to see us," they were taken to the royal chambers.

"We found the Indian prince there," said Vasco, "and he reclined on a couch covered with green velvet, over which had been flung a dazzling white sheet which was finer than any linen. He was chewing betel and in his hand held a large golden cup to spit into. At his side stood a golden basin so large that a man could hardly encircle it with his arms. This held the sliced betel nuts."

Vasco saluted him by clasping his hands together and lifting them on high, and the zamorin replied by offering him jacks (a Polynesian fruit) and ripe bananas.

After that he asked the captain major what had brought him to Calicut.

"I am the ambassador of the King of Portugal," said Vasco, "who is the lord of many other lands too. And I do not come to seek silver and gold, for in our land there is so much of both that the king does not seek any more. But for sixty years we have heard of a king in these parts who worships the same God as we and now we have found him." (Vasco still thought the Hindus were Christians.) "I bear letters from my sovereign to this king. They say the King of Portugal desires to be his friend and brother."

"I desire to be his friend and brother, too," replied the zamorin.

"Will you send ambassadors to him?"

"I will send ambassadors."

Then the zamorin bade his servants to see to it that the Portuguese were fed again and given lodgings for the night. This was fortunate, for soon a monsoon rain began to pour down and the streets flooded. But not before the bedazzled seafarers were taken, by the light of four-wicked blazing torches, to the carpeted house of a wealthy Moor.

Unhappily, however, the good will of the zamorin did not last for long. There were two reasons. Dom Manoel had ordered Vasco to present gifts to any native prince he found, but since up until that time the Portuguese had dealt only with poor and backward people, the gifts Vasco brought with him were hardly fine enough to impress an Oriental potentate who was far richer than Dom Manoel! Vasco gave the zamorin twelve pieces of *lambel*—a cheap and gaudy striped cloth popular with jungle dwellers—four scarlet hoods, six Portuguese hats, four strings of coral, two barrels of oil, and two casks of honey.

Through his scornful officials, the zamorin laughed at this parsimony. "Why, the poorest merchant from Mecca could do better!" one of them said. "Even the meanest wretch from the barren and starving Persian Gulf land of the fish eaters!"

But the second reason was even more persuasive. For as long as anyone could remember, the spice trade, which was the richest trade of all, had been in the hands of the Arabs who had loaded everything from cardamom to cloves into their not always seaworthy ships and carried it to the Red Sea. From there it was taken overland to Cairo, where it was sold at a great profit mainly to traders from Europe.

Now the Arabs saw a threat to their monopoly. They would surely lose some of the trade. They might lose all of it.

So they set out to poison the mind of the zamorin.

"These men will come, take what you give them, then go, and you will never see them again. But we bring you riches year after year."

The King of the Seacoast was convinced, and thereupon harassment followed harassment. The small amount of merchandise Vasco had brought with him was impounded, and some of his men were detained, and even Vasco himself for two terrible nights! He was released only after sending a secret message to the men still aboard his ships to load and train their guns. Then with black looks he threatened to have them turn on the zamorin. That did the trick. But his men were still prisoners, and most of the Calicut merchandise he had been promised was never delivered. Exorbitant customs dues were imposed on what little was. Indeed, complete disaster threatened.

It would have struck if Vasco had not acted.

Masking his anger and annoyance, the captain major sent word from his ship that he was eager to buy precious stones and that anyone who had any to offer should bring them to his ship. Twenty-five would-be vendors appeared. He promptly seized them.

"I will release them when my men are set free," he told the zamorin.

Since among those Vasco had seized there were many important and wealthy Calicut citizens, the King of the Seacoast had no choice but to comply. He released the Portuguese and Vasco set free the Indians.

All but six of them, that is.

"These I will take to Portugal," he said. "When they have seen our land, I can send them back as ambassadors."

This was on August 28, and on August 29, the Portuguese ships weighed anchor.

"On that day, we set sail for Portugal, greatly rejoicing in our good fortune at having made so great a discovery," said Vasco.

And now, more than a year later—and after hardships and dangers that were even greater than those encountered on the outward voyage—he stood in Limoeiro Palace and talked to his sovereign.

"I have tried to obey your commands, Your Majesty. I have not done all that I wished to do—or that you commanded—but I have done much. Of the spices and splendid things of the land, I have at least brought samples, and now that I have shown the way, other men can return, better provided than I, and bring back riches in quantity. And they will have with them men who can guide them, and who, being of the land, can deal better with the zamorin than I did. They can tell him that Portugal is a friend and he will believe them. I hope that I have done well, Your Majesty."

"You have done more than well," replied Manoel, "and soon every man in the land shall know it."

Vasco, he said, would henceforth be Dom Vasco da Gama, and would be given the lordship of Sines, his birthplace, if the Order of São Tiago could be persuaded to yield its rights in the place. (They were not persuaded, but Vasco was given a pension of 1000 *cruzados*, the right to invest 200 *cruzados* annually in any trade with India, the rank of Admiral of India, and later the title of Count of Vidigueira).

"The world will know too," Dom Manoel added.

The Portuguese monarch at once took the title of "Dom Manoel, King of Portugal and of the Algarves on this side of and beyond the sea (southern Portugal and Ceuta), Lord of Guinea in Africa (the West African land discovered by Henry's captains and their successors), and Lord of the Conquest, the Commerce, and the Navigation of Ethiopia, Arabia, Persia, and India," and wrote to kings and cardinals, dukes, emperors, and doges, triumphantly announcing "the good news."

Venice, whose monopoly of the rich trade of the Indies was at stake, got the tidings first. Indeed, even before Vasco talked to his king, the Venetian government had received a disturbing letter from one of its agents in Cairo.

"Three ships of Portugal," it said, "under the command

of Christopher Columbus [!] have put into Aden and Calicut seeking information on spices in the islands. Fortunately, two were wrecked and the third leaked so badly it could not return."

"I simply do not believe it!" cried a Venetian merchant, and he was right, for Columbus was in the West Indies, not in Calicut.

But the merchant had to believe the official message that followed: "We have found the road to India. Send your galleys to Lisbon if you want spices."

So, too, did the Florentine bankers and the Genoese shipmen, and the merchants of the Low Countries, Germany, France, England, Denmark, and even Poland. Into the city on the Tagus they poured. "All of us," said one who came from beyond the Rhine, "were eager to take advantage of the golden opportunities there."

As a result, almost overnight Lisbon became the most feverishly active place in Europe. Its squares and its streets, the taverns of its waterside *ribeira* district, and the inns of its Alfama quarter, teemed with an ever growing multitude. They were of all sorts—Portuguese and foreigners, careful traders and reckless speculators, men willing to work and lounging idlers, rich men and poor men, beggarmen and thieves, and even women and children, all of them listening openmouthed to tales of India and the journey there, told to them by returning sailors who did not have to embroider their stories, since the truth was strange enough.

From the city gates to Restello, a swarm of carpenters toiled night and day constructing palaces and villas on every hilltop and hillside. Another swarm were hard at work on the slowly rising Cathedral do Mar and the Hieronymite monastery nearer the shore. A third swarm built too many warehouses to number where not long before there had been yellow sands.

The shipyards were also busy night and day building new ships, and repairing those that had returned—and so too were the swordmakers and the gunsmiths and the armorers. "The forges of the armorers," said a visitor, "seemed like one-eyed cyclopes working in the smithy of Vulcan."

Even the day-to-day business of a still-medieval city went on at an increased pace, for the mills—their weary horses plodding eternally—had to turn without ceasing to provide all the flour now needed, while the water sellers with their stone jugs, the wine sellers with their goatskin flasks, and the sellers of meat, fish, and oil, of cabbages, turnips, melons, olives, strawberries, and other fruits and vegetables could not even begin to keep up with the demands of their customers.

How could they? There was hardly anyone in Lisbon from king to alley-haunting cutthroat who did not have coin in his purse—coin put there by Vasco da Gama and his voyage to the East, this latest and most dramatic adventure of the men who, inspired by Henry, had gone down to the sea in ships.

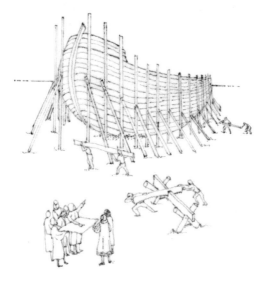

The Navigator Who Never Sailed a Ship

Man has not always been a seafaring animal and someone has even suggested that the first person to make a voyage afloat was swept into a river by a flood, and then saved his life by clinging to a log.

The next step was to fashion a boat. This was first done by lopping off the branches of some mighty oak tree and then hollowing out its trunk. The dugout was followed by the raft, and then came the reed canoe, the skin-covered coracle, and finally, even before the dawn of history, the true ship with keel, ribs, and wooden planking.

At least one archaeologist has insisted that some of these primitive craft traveled very far indeed. "It is probable," he writes, "that the neolithic Scandinavians"—men still in the Stone Age—"were skilled navigators, and that they reached North America some thousands of years before the Norsemen."

However, for the most part, in those ancient days men only sailed coastal waters or nearby lakes and rivers. Indeed, the first recorded long voyages did not take place until around 2600 B.C. At that time, Egyptian ships equipped with oars were plying regularly both to Asia Minor and up and down the Red Sea. Then in 1492 B.c. they ventured on a real voyage of discovery. In that year, Queen Hatshepsut, wishing to show that a woman pharaoh could accomplish as much as a man, sent a fleet of forty vessels to Punt, a mysterious African land which may have been as far south as the mouth of the Zambezi River. There the Egyptians entertained the native king and queen (she was so grossly fat that she must have suffered from elephantiasis) with bread, ale, wine, meat, and dried fruit. In return the Egyptians were allowed to bring back gum, incense, ebony, gold, mascara, dog-headed and long-tailed monkeys, and even a few slaves.

"No other ruler has done the like!" cried Hatshepsut. "My ships have found the land of Gods! But why not? I am the daughter of the god, Ammon-Ra!"

It was not long before the Egyptians were followed by others. By the Phoenicians—called in Egypt "the bronze men from the north"—who, some say, took to the sea even before the Egyptians did. By the Minoans, who lived on Crete, and were ruled by their famous thalassocrats, or sea kings. By King Solomon, whose ships, built by King Hiram of Tyre, went to Ophir in southern Arabia. By the Greeks, and, finally, by the Carthaginians and the Romans.

Working their way from headland to headland and from cape to cape, for they rarely sailed out of sight of land, all these people went to much of the world known to them. The Phoenicians ranged along North Africa to the Pillars of Melkarth (the Straits of Gibraltar). In the latter place, they founded Gades (Cádiz) and established trade with rich barbarian Tartessus (Biblical Tarshish at the mouth of the Guadalquivir) for its lead, iron, tin, and silver. The Minoans not only ruled the eastern Mediterranean from Crete to the site of Venice, but had trading posts in distant Sardinia. The Greeks founded Massilia (Marseille), Parthenope (Naples), Rhegion (Reggio),

Croton, Tarentum, Messina, Gela, Syracuse, and Panormum (Palermo). To these places went their sturdy ships of "twenty oars and mast of pine set into a hole in the cross plank,"— this is how they are described by Homer in the *Odyssey*— each heavily laden with ample provisions of barley meal and "wine in well-sewn skins." They also sent their vessels to the farther shores of the Pontus Axeinos (the Unfriendly Sea, our Black Sea), where they established cities at the mouths of the Don and the Dniester rivers in southern Russia and in the lofty Caucasus.

But even that did not mark the limit of ancient voyaging.

Around 450 B.C. the Greek geographer Herodotus visited Egypt, and there heard an amazing tale. About 150 years earlier, he was told, Pharaoh Necho II summoned one of his captains and bade him assemble a fleet and with it circumnavigate Africa. He was to sail south from the Red Sea, then west, then north, returning through the Straits of Gibraltar.

"This," said Herodotus, "I was informed he did. He set out as commanded, and as often as autumn came, he and his men went ashore and sowed the land and waited until harvest time. Then they gathered the crop and went on again. Two years elapsed this way, and in the third year, they sailed through the Pillars of Hercules (the Straits of Gibraltar) and came to Egypt once more.

"Of course," Herodotus went on, "I do not believe this, for they said too many incredible things. For example, they said that as they sailed toward the west the sun was to their right. This is impossible."

But if they sailed west in the southern hemisphere, the sun *had* to be to their right, and so what made the story unbelievable to Herodotus is the very thing that makes us think it was probably true.

The ancients also made another remarkable African voyage —and this one we know was actually made.

At just about the time that Herodotus was in Egypt, the suffetes (rulers) of the Carthaginian Republic gave one of its admirals, Hanno, a fleet of fifty pentaconters (fifty-oared galleys) with thirty thousand men, women, and children aboard them. His orders were to skirt the coast of West Africa until he found a suitable place, and there to set up a Carthaginian colony.

This Hanno attempted to do. He passed through the Straits of Gibraltar and crawled down the coast of Morocco, where he saw elephants and other African animals in the swamps at the mouth of one of its rivers. He established his first settlement at Cerne, an island off the Spanish Sahara which cannot be identified today, and then continued until he reached the mouth of the Sénégal. He pushed up the river until he reached mountains, "which rose like towers," and encountered wild men clad in skins who attacked him with stones.

Thus greeted, he returned to Cerne, but not for long. Shortly he sailed southward again for twelve days, always skirting the land, encountering strange people "whose tongue was unintelligible" and often seeing crocodiles and hippopotamuses. "On the last day of the twelve," Hanno says, "we made fast under a high, wooded range, with varied and fragrant trees." This was Cape Verde.

But not even Cape Verde marked the end of Hanno's journey. He rounded the cape and then continued, past the estuary of the Gambia, until he came to another great promontory, which he called the Western Horn.

"Here we could see many fires being kindled, and at night we heard the noise of pipes and cymbals, the din of tom-toms, and the shouts of a multitude of people; so we sailed away in fear. Four days later, we again saw land. It was ablaze at night, and in the center, a leaping flame towered above the others and seemed to reach the stars. This was the highest mountain we saw. It was called the Chariot of the Gods."

Almost certainly the mountain was Mount Cameroon, 13,353 feet high and located where the coast turns south again just beyond the southeasternmost point of what is today Nigeria. It is the only active volcano in West Africa. To be sure, it is a twelve-, not four-, day journey from Cape Verde, but Hanno's account was not written until he had returned to Carthage, and by then he may well have forgotten just how long this stage of his voyage took.

After this, he went on for three days more until he came upon a small island filled with wild people. "By far the greater number were women with hairy bodies. Our interpreters called them gorillas." Hanno thought them humans, but they were probably chimpanzees. "We could not catch any of the men, for they scampered up the steep rocks and pelted us with stones. But we did capture three women. However, they bit and scratched and resisted us. So we killed them and skinned them and brought their hides to Carthage. At that point we ended our voyage, for we had run out of provisions."

The men of olden days explored the north too, and one of them, Pytheas, a Greek from Marseille, wrote a book about his travels. It was called *About the Ocean*, and has been a source of argument ever since.

Pytheas was a geographer and a very good astronomer, but he was also a tin-and-amber-merchant, and according to his story, set out in 325 B.C. to discover a new route to the Casseritides, or Tin Islands. (Actually they were not islands but the Cornish mainland.) So as not to be stopped by Carthaginian vessels guarding the Straits of Gibraltar, the first part of his voyage was overland. He went up the Rhone and then across Gaul (France) to the site of today's Brest. There he sailed in one of the sturdy ships of the Veneti, seafaring inhabitants of Brittany, to Land's End on the tip of Cornwall. Even though he'd reached his goal, he continued up the west coast of Britain past Ierne (Ireland), through the Hebudes (the Hebrides), and to the Orcades (the Orkneys).

The most adventurous part of his travels was still to come. Over stormy and fog-wreathed seas he worked his way north for five days before grounding on an island lost in the gray mist. He called it Thule (it was either Iceland or the upper Norwegian coast) and said it was "the outermost part of the earth." This done, he returned to Britain again, went down its east coast, and crossed the North Sea to sail along the north-west shores of the Netherlands and Germany and perhaps even into the Baltic.

Pytheas came home by way of the Rhine and began to talk. Pandemonium broke out.

"Not even the god Mercury could have traveled all the miles he said he did!" cried one who listened to him.

"Charlatan!" exclaimed another. "Everything he says is a tissue of falsehoods and his only aim is to attract attention as a juggler does!"

It is not hard to see why they felt this way. One might be-lieve that there were places so bleak and chilly that neither wheat nor cattle could be raised, and the natives had to live on oats, wild honey, and wild berries. This was certainly true of Scotland and Thule. One might believe—for the Greeks liked to look with scorn upon the barbarians—that even in southern Britain the inhabitants dwelt in huts made of wattles smeared with mud, and that because of the continual rain they had to thresh their grain indoors and store it in underground silos. One might believe that they drank mead or beer instead of civilized wine.

But more about the twelve-foot tides that came rushing up and down the French and British rivers? (We know now, of course, that there are forty-foot tides in Brittany and in parts of Britain.)

What about seas running eighty cubits (at least 120 feet) high to the north of Scotland? (It is common knowledge today that in the Pentland Firth when a gale runs against a tidal race, the waves are sometimes as high as sixty feet and throw solid spray more than twice that.)

What about Pytheas's famous sea-lung "by which air and earth and sea are bound together in conglomerate mass"? (This may have been the fog over floe ice.) And his statement that at Thule in June and July the night lasted only two hours, and that farther north, "the sun at midsummer never set at all"? Or that beyond Thule, the sea was frozen solid? Who could believe this?

Pytheas was not the only ancient mariner who knew about the Atlantic. Greek mythology is filled with tales of islands to the west where the sun shone long after it had set in Greece, and where, in the gardens of the Hesperides, golden apples (possibly oranges) hung from every bough and the springs flowed with life-giving nectar instead of water. The philosopher Plato also told of the island Atlantis, far out in the ocean, which because of the wickedness of its inhabitants, one day sank, leaving only its peaks above the sea. Atlantis, his contemporaries thought, was in the Atlantic, and the peaks were the legendary Isles of the Blest.

The Greeks and the Romans and the Carthaginians sailed to the islands they thought were the Isles of the Blest. In fact, they were the Canaries, just off northwest Africa, and, possibly, Madeira. The Greek historian Diodorus (about 100 B.C.) tells of a Carthaginian ship that was blown to sea and, after several days of sailing, came upon an island with fertile plains, well-wooded mountains, and a perfect climate. It was as warm in winter as in summer. The Roman general Sertorius wished to retire there when he was defeated in Spain.

These sailors of old may have gone even farther. About the same time that Hanno was going down the west coast of

Africa, another Carthaginian, Himilco, sailed west until he came to a place of calms, shoals, tangled seaweed, and curious sea monsters. Later he discovered ten islands. Was the place of shoals and seaweeds the Sargasso Sea and were the islands the Azores? (As a matter of fact, it is said that in 1749, a hoard of gold coins stamped with the horse or horse's head used by Carthage was discovered on Corvo, one of the westernmost of this group. The coins have since disappeared.) Even more remarkable, it was reported by a Greek writer that some time before A.D. 170, a ship belonging to one Euphemius of Caria had been blown across the ocean to an island inhabited by men with red skin who wore horse's tails on their heads and did not have any morals. When the Spaniards came to the Antilles, many centuries later, it seemed to them that the natives answered this description in every way. Recently an American scholar, Dr. Cyrus Gordon, claimed that Phoenician mariners had reached South America in the sixth century B.C. He said that one of the ships sent to circumnavigate Africa by Necho II was blown off its course, and with twelve men and three women, came, in the words of a stone tablet supposedly found in Brazil in 1872, to a "distant shore, a land of mountains." This stone has disappeared too, but if it told a true story then America was discovered two thousand years before Columbus.

Finally the Greeks and then the Romans sailed the Indian Ocean. That wide body—and the fact that its farther shores were the source of the gums and aromatics they sought so eagerly—had been known since at least 325 B.C., when Alexander the Great sent a fleet under one of his captains, Nearchus, from the mouth of the Indus to the mouth of the Euphrates. But they did not sail the ocean regularly until the discovery of the southwest monsoons around 110 B.C. by a Greek pilot named Hippalus. He not only discovered them, but gave his name to them. From then on, they were known as the Hippalus winds.

After that, travel eastward was almost on ocean-liner sched-
ule. It took twenty days to go from Puteoli (Pozzuoli near
Naples) to Alexandria; from Alexandria to Coptos (Quift
today) up the Nile, twelve days; from Coptos to Berenice on
the Red Sea (here the traveler and his goods moved on camel
back), twelve days; from Berenice to India (now on a ship
again), seventy days. The whole trip took one hundred fourteen days. Allowing for time to trade and barter, a round trip
could be made in approximately one year.

But the Romans—and the Greeks who served them—did not
end their travels east there. More than a few of them pushed
on to the Maldive Islands far out in the Indian Ocean, and
to Taprobane (Ceylon) and then to the Andaman Islands, the
Nicobar Islands, and Malaysia. A Greek merchant sailed across
the Gulf of Siam to Cambodia and possibly to Haiphong,
and Roman coins have been found in the Mekong Delta. The
Romans even went to China—Sinae, the fabled silk land.
In A.D. 166 Antun (this was the Chinese name for Marcus
Aurelius) sent an official embassy to Huan-ti, the Chinese
emperor. He received it graciously, although he haughtily
called the gifts the Roman ambassador brought him a tribute.

But as Rome fell and the Dark Ages began, all this came to
an end. The Arabs poured out of the desert and conquered
Egypt, thus cutting Europe off from its ancient prosperous
trade with the East. Then they spread out until they controlled
all of North Africa and most of Portugal and Spain. From one
end of the Mediterranean to the other they ended western
shipping as it had been in Roman days.

They also cut off the Atlantic by the stories they spread
about it. They told horrendous tales about this "green sea
of darkness," as they called it. It was filled, one Arab said,
with strange and terrifying beasts, and it ended in a roaring
cloud of steam as it poured over the precipice at the edge of
the world.

The barbarians of the north wrought equal havoc. Tribe after tribe moved into the rich lands that once were Roman. They did little but plunder and burn. The cities which once sent out ship after ship were soon in ruins.

They destroyed Roman civilization too—Roman law and order, and Roman and Greek learning. It is not possible to be law abiding when one has to live with little but rapine and murder. It is not possible to study and learn when one's every energy is devoted to survival. Ignorance, therefore, soon took the place of knowledge. Nowhere was this more true than in the realm of geography. Just to take one example, the Greeks had discovered that the world was round long before the birth of Christ, and by 200 B.C. one of their philosophers, Eratosthenes, had calculated its circumference. He was wrong by only fifty miles. But now, in the Dark Ages, most men—including some scholars and almost all sea captains—believed once again that it was flat. And who wants to risk sailing over the edge of a flat world?

This does not mean, of course, that no one ventured onto the high seas at all. The Irish tell tall tales of their St. Brendan, who with seventeen companions sailed out into the Atlantic in little currachs. If we can believe these tales, they not only reached the Faeroe Islands and Iceland, where they saw Mount Hekla erupting—we do know for a fact that Irish monks visited both—but crossed the ocean to an Island of the Saints, with shoals where darting fish swam in crystal-clear waters. This, say St. Brendan's admirers, was in the Caribbean.

Idrisi, the Arab geographer, has a story of the Lisbon wanderers whose explorations probably took place between 1048 and 1147. Eight in all, these Maghurin, as they were called, set out before an east wind; reached an area of thick seaweed and foul odors; turned south to El Ghanam (possibly Madeira), an island where they found herds of sheep whose flesh was too bitter to eat; and finally came to another island which had houses and cultivated fields on it. It was probably one of the Canaries. Here they were seized and taken to the king, who found a way of asking them who they were and what they were seeking.

"We come from Leixbona [Lisbon]," they replied, "and we are seeking the ends of the ocean and its wonders."

The king laughed at this. "You are great fools," he said. "Why, look you, my father once sent some slaves to do the same, and after they had sailed for a month, they found themselves where there was neither sun, nor moon, nor stars, and so they returned without results." He then told the eight that since they had stumbled upon his realm and did not come to conquer it, he would merely keep them prisoners until a west wind blew.

"When it does, I will blindfold you and put you in a boat again."

This he did, and three days after they and some of the king's men had embarked they reached Africa.

"There they were put ashore with their hands bound," concluded Idrisi, "and shortly afterward, they were freed by Berbers, who returned them to their native city. There is still a street in Lisbon named after them."

It is also almost certain that the Northmen island-hopped from Iceland to Greenland to North America around A.D. 1000. But at the time this was not known outside of the north.

For the most part, however, European seamen were content to stay close to home and used the seas only to make a modest living. The Venetians, for instance, carried salt, and the Sardinians and the Spaniards and the Portuguese, who were gradually freeing themselves from Arab control, fished for tunny. They were content to go back to creeping from one familiar headland to another. They gave up sailing the open seas.

Fortunately, however, the Dark Ages did not last forever—

at most, for six or seven hundred years. Then men began to venture forth again.

In 1291 Tedisio Doria of Genoa, accompanied by the Vivaldi brothers, who were ship builders, sailed down the coast of Africa looking, they said, for India. Camel-riding Bedouins saw them sailing past Cape Juby, but they were never heard of again.

In 1312, Lanzarotto Malocelo, also from Genoa, rediscovered the Canaries, and these islands were visited again in 1341 by Florentine merchants, who told their story to the famous writer Boccaccio. By 1402, Frenchmen from Dieppe had briefly occupied them, although they later sold their rights to Castile.

European seamen were increasingly well-equipped for this outburst of boldness, for the new age—its very name, Renaissance, means "rebirth"—brought with it a revival of every kind of mental activity, science—including the science of navigation—as well as art, philosophy, and writing.

No one knows who invented the compass. Some say the ancient Chinese. But as early as 1187, an Englishman, Neckam, told of a needle "which swings on a point and shows the direction of the north." And although eighty-one years later Dante's teacher, Brunetto Latini, said that no one dared use this compass "for fear of being thought a magician," by 1300 an Amalfi sea captain had put it into a box so that it could be used on shipboard. By the time Boccaccio's merchants came to the Canaries, few vessels sailed without one.

The astrolabe, an instrument for measuring the height above the horizon of the sun or a star, had been known to the ancients, but it was now simplified and improved for use on shipboard. For rough-and-ready use, the Jacob's staff—a long stick with a movable crosspiece—had been available since 1342.

Portolanos—up-to-date and improved versions of ancient sailing directions, such as *The Periplus of the Erythrean* (*Red*)

Sea written in 90 B.C.—came into being in quantity, and now were in the cabin of almost every mariner. One of the most famous of these gave useful information about every seaport, big or little, from Cádiz to the Irish Sea in one direction and to the Greek islands in the other. Maps became available too. Many of them were crisscrossed with lines showing the direction from place to place. The portolanos gave the distances.

Finally, the ships themselves were better. Long out of date was the clumsy and unmanageable one-masted vessel steered by an oar. Now vessels had many masts and were steered by a perpendicular rudder hung from pintles on the stern. Cried that doughty old knight, the Lord of Joinville, as he sailed on a crusade with the French king, Saint Louis: "Why, they can be guided from right to left as one guides a horse!"

As men turned to the sea again, these advances were nowhere better put to use than in the little country which we now call Portugal. It is not difficult to see why the Portuguese were a seafaring people. Although one third of their land is fit for the plow, the rest of it consists of mountains, crags, forests, and moors. Like ancient Greece and like Phoenicia, which faces a desert, Portugal did not have enough arable land to support a growing population. Fortunately, however, it had a long coast line with many beaches and not a few good harbors. Its people, too, had seafaring blood in their veins. The original inhabitants, the Celtiberi (a mixture of golden-haired Celts from Gaul and dark-haired Spanish Iberians), had mingled with newcomers such as the Phoenicians, Greeks, Carthaginians, and even the Moors. All of these were or became seafarers. The Portuguese, then, were seamen by inheritance as well as need.

At first, to be sure, they were only coastal seamen, but soon they ventured farther and farther afield. This was especially true after the Moors had been driven from all but Portugal's extreme south by the middle of the twelfth century. There was a Portuguese factory (trading post) in Bruges as early as the twelfth century, and by the thirteenth there were Portuguese in almost every French seaport. At that time, they also began to trade with England. In the year 1226 alone, one hundred safe conducts were granted to Portuguese merchants doing business in London. In the fourteenth century, Lisbon was made a free port. After that, as many as five hundred ships could often be seen anchored before it. Some were foreign—for trade must go both ways—but most were Portuguese.

As the Portuguese traded, their kings also created a Portuguese navy. It is not known exactly when it first sailed the seas, but during the reign of Affonso Henriques (1128–1185), Portugal's second ruler and her first king, the navy was strong enough to disperse a Moorish fleet near the mouth of the Tagus.

Sancho II (1223–1245) and Affonso III (1245–1279) sent their vessels around Cape St. Vincent to help crusaders from the north capture Silves and Faro, towns on the southern Portuguese coast. Even Denis the Farmer (*Diniz o Lavrador*) (1279–1325), turned from his wheatlands and vineyards long enough to think about the sea. Not only did he agree to a suggestion made by the merchants themselves that he tax their exports "for God's service and the good of the land" and use the money to build and maintain the fleets they needed for protection; he also ordered a large pine forest to be planted. It was to extend from Leiria, north of his capital, to the seacoast. It was said that this *Pinhal del Rey* was to hold back the wind-driven sand dunes. But it was also to provide masts and timber for Denis's ships.

In 1323 the Portuguese appointed as high admiral one Emanuele Pazagno of Genoa, a hereditary lord whom they promptly renamed Manoel Pesanha. In return for pay and privileges, he and his heirs agreed to see to it that Portugal always had twenty *sabedores do mar* (trained sea captains) to command her galleys and keep her strong afloat.

But even though Portugal had turned seaward almost as soon as she became an independent land, it was not until a new dynasty began its rule that she embarked on the adventures which would make her one of the greatest seafaring nations in history.

John of Avis (King João I) had never expected to sit on the Portuguese throne. He had no reason to. To be sure, he was the son of King Pedro I, but he was illegitimate, and when his half brother, Fernando, put on the crown, Fernando was only twenty-two years old. But Fernando died at thirty-eight, leaving as his only heir a daughter married to a Castilian prince who forthwith proclaimed himself King of Portugal. At this the Portuguese rose in their wrath and they offered the throne to João. He accepted it with gusto.

This was on April 6, 1385, and on August 14 of the same year, with his valiant constable Nun'Álvares Pereira at his right hand, João routed an invading Castilian army at Aljubarrota. In this battle he was aided by John of Gaunt, uncle of King Richard II of England. John sent five hundred English men-and-arms and archers to fight beside João. A little more than a year later, the king married John's daughter Philippa. He was twenty-nine. She was twenty-one.

Their reign was distinguished in every way. João—said by a modern historian to be "not a genius, but able and efficient" —was a brave soldier, an intelligent statesman, and a very shrewd judge of men. Philippa, an English beauty with wheat-gold hair, a delicate pink-and-white complexion, thin red lips, and clear blue eyes, had, in addition to her charms, a high English sense of duty and morality.

Between them, they transformed the kingdom. João defended the frontiers against the Castilians, who although defeated, would not surrender; he finally forced them to pay a war indemnity of 80,000 *dobras*, and to make peace with him. Philippa reformed the court. No longer could a king slay his ladylove's murderers with his own hands as Pedro had, nor could a prince—even João had done this before his marriage to Philippa—abscond with a beautiful dark-eyed peasant maid and carry her off to his castle. Lisbon and Oporto and Coimbra —for there was no one royal residence—became models for all Europe.

João and Philippa did one other thing. They brought into being one of the most remarkable royal families that the world has ever known.

They had eight children and—this itself was extraordinary in those days—six of them lived to maturity: Duarte, born in 1391; Pedro, born in 1392; Henrique (Henry the Navigator), born in 1394; Isabella, born in 1397; João, born in 1400; and Fernando, born in 1402. With the exception of João, every one of them played an important role in his nation's, if not the world's, history.

Duarte (Edward) would be king himself and thus continue the line that ruled Portugal until 1578. Yellow-haired Pedro, who looked like an English lord, would win renown both as a scholar and a world traveler. Dom Fernando, the youngest brother, would display a moral courage that was even greater than his older brothers' courage in the field of action. Isabella, who was to marry a foreign prince, Philip, Duke of Burgundy, would accomplish just about as much as a woman could in those days. Something of a prude and *béguine* (a much too devout woman), she reformed the Burgundian court, much as her mother had reformed Portugal, yet still left it one of the most magnificent in Europe.

But of all the six—the five brothers and one sister—the one who is rightfully best remembered is the third brother, Henry.

His friend, the chronicler Azurara, describes Henry in the full flush of his mature manhood.

"This nobleman," he says, "was of a good height and had a sturdy frame. He was big, and strong of limb, and the hair of his head was somewhat erect. Its color was fair when he was born, but constant toil and exposure had turned it dark. His expression at first sight inspired fear in those who did not know him, and when angry, his countenance was harsh."

This man who never commanded a vessel looked like a typical sea captain. This can be confirmed by anyone who looks at his portrait, which hangs in the Museum of Ancient Art in Lisbon. In it, his brow is wrinkled as if he were studying the waters in front of him. His eyes seem to be piercing the fog.

And Henry had qualities that went with his appearance.

"Strength of heart and keenness of mind he had to a very high degree," Azurara continues, "and beyond any other man, he was ambitious of achieving great and lofty deeds, nor was he ever avaricious or close-fisted in moving toward his objectives. Indeed, his palace was a school of hospitality for those both native and foreign who told him what he wanted to know. Few of them went away from him without a reward. He was a man of great wisdom and had a good memory. He was steadfast in adversity and humble in prosperity."

Most of all, like most great men, he had a single goal, although he did not realize what this goal was until he had attained full manhood. When he did, he pursued it as the Knights of the Round Table sought after the Holy Grail. To attain it, he sacrificed everything, including some things dear to him: his sleep—"it would be hard to tell how many nights he passed when his eyes never closed," says Azurara—his peace of mind, his health. Some say he even sacrificed two of his brothers. But in the end, he attained his goal—to the benefit of all mankind.

A Knight Errant in Africa

We know nothing of Prince Henry's babyhood and boyhood, except that he had a nurse, Mécia Lourenço, a good and religious woman, and that one of his tutors was her husband, Dom Lopo Dias, a member of the Order of Christ. We know little more about his youth, but there is much we can surmise about it. Henry and his brothers were princes, and in those days, princes were far from being figureheads. This was an accepted fact, and in every country in Europe, the king's eldest son was taught that he would one day sit on his father's throne, his brothers that they must dutifully aid him and counsel him. Thus Portugal's *infantes* would have been taught everything it was thought necessary, in those days, for a prince to know.

They would have been taught, for example, to love the outdoors. This would make them hardy and resolute. A king's son should be both. As soon as they were able to walk they would have been placed upon gentle steeds and then fiery ones. All of them, we know, became expert riders, and Duarte even wrote a book on horsemanship. They would have been taught to draw the English bow, aim the arbalest (a heavy medieval crossbow), wield the sword, hurl a javelin, and wrestle. They would have been taught early to hawk, and to hunt—even the bad-tempered, dangerous Portuguese wild boar.

They would have been taught, too, to eat and drink sparingly so as to build up their endurance. This they did. It was said of Henry, for example, that he could ride forty leagues and back in a day and a night without pausing to rest. One hundred and twenty miles! And his brothers could do almost as much.

They were also taught to study. As the revival of learning began in Italy and spread throughout Europe, it was no longer enough for a prince or a nobleman or a knight to be brawny and brave. He must also be able to read and understand what he had read, and also to write. They inherited a gift for both. Their grandfather, John of Gaunt, was as renowned as a patron of letters as he was skillful in arms. As a matter of fact, the English poet Geoffrey Chaucer was John's brother-in-law, and thus the Portuguese princes' great-uncle by marriage.

The princes not only learned to read their own language and to love Portugal's plaintive poetry, some of the best of which, it so happens, was written by Portuguese kings. They had reading knowledge of every important European language, and Duarte and Pedro—and possibly Henry—learned to translate what they read into Portuguese. They thus became familiar with the finest medieval literature, from Dante, who wrote movingly about Hell, Heaven, and the island of Purgatory (which Dante seems to place somewhere in one of the oceans which Portuguese mariners soon would be sailing) to Guido delle Colonne, who told the story of Helen of Troy in Latin.

They also studied philosophy, mathematics, astronomy, and geography. Henry in especial studied the latter. He read every medieval geography he could lay his hands on, only to discover that for the most part they told only of mermaids or monsters and monopodes (men with only one leg), and left the real world undescribed. Then he turned to the ancients—Herodotus, Ptolemy, Strabo, and Pliny. These men, he found, had a more scientific approach, and they at least told him about the lands they or men they had talked to had visited.

But even they had some strange ideas, and frequently left out as much as they put in. What about the distant east? Men were beginning to hear tales of it again. What about the north (Thule and Scandinavia), left hidden in the mist since the days of Pytheas? What about the mysterious western ocean? What—and this would grow more important to Henry every year and every day—about the sultry south?

The brothers also learned how to conduct themselves as the ruling family of their father's kingdom, and Duarte, how to be the first man of this ruling family. Still boys, they were compelled to sit long hours when the king's council convened. This was boring indeed—especially when the sun shone out of a blue Portuguese sky, and a breeze blew in the fragrance of flowers and the sound of bird song. But they had to sit there just the same.

Finally, they were taught that they must always stand together. "This is the story of the English arrow," said their mother, Queen Philippa. "One of them you can break easily, but if you bind many of them together, it is beyond your strength to break them."

Evidently the princes heeded her words—at any rate as long as they were growing up—for Duarte was able to say that "never was there any jealousy among us."

"We put up with each other's idiosyncrasies," he added. With people of such individuality, this was not always easy to do.

But full as their days were, they were not full enough and the princes still had time to dream. Most of their dreams were of knightly adventure. This is not surprising, for they lived in a knightly age. It was the age of Sir Thomas Malory, who wrote *Le Morte d'Arthur* and gave us most of our stories of King Arthur, Camelot, and the Knights of the Round Table. Malory was well known in Portugal. It was also the age of the princes' uncle, Prince Edward of Wales, who was known as the Black Prince. He helped win the battle of Crécy and himself won the battle of Poitiers. In this battle, he took the King of France prisoner. The Black Prince is considered to be one of the greatest of all English soldiers. The young princes were told of his skill and valor, and how in his youth he had defied the same French king he later made captive. The latter had arrogantly summoned him to Paris. "Since you have sent for us," the prince replied, "we come gladly. But it will be with basinets on our head and with sixty thousand followers."

They heard songs and stories about the heroes of old and about modern heroes: Roland, whose horn sounded in the pass of Roncesvalles where he died with Olivier and Archbishop Turpin; Spanish Ruy Diaz de Bivar, called el Cid Campeador; Portuguese Geraldo Sempavor (Gerald the Fearless); French Bertrand Du Guesclin; English—though he and his White Company fought in Italy—Sir John Hawkwood; and Italian Sforza Attendolo.

They also heard the often-repeated tale of how Nun'Álvares had helped their father win his kingdom. Although Nun' was later beatified by the Church, at that time he was thought of only as a mighty warrior.

The Portuguese princes longed to emulate these men—especially their father and Nun'. But how? They consulted together—Duarte and Pedro and Henry, for Dom João and Dom Fernando were still only boys—and then asked their father to send them forth to war.

"We are of an age to be made knights," they told him, "but what would knighthood be worth if it were not won with swords and spurs?"

King João listened attentively.

"I will give you a year of tournaments instead," he said. "From every kingdom in Christendom, I will invite all the noble lords and gentlemen who by age and character deserve the honor. And I will order festive days during which there will be great tournaments and jousts followed by magnificent banquets at which rich gifts will be given. You will take part in all these, and at the end I will make you knights."

"That would be well if we were a merchant's sons," the princes objected, "for they think that the more money spent on a business the greater it is. But we are a king's sons."

"But where will you find the war you seek?" João asked. "Certainly not near at hand, for after ten years we are at peace with our neighbors. We must stay at peace."

The king's treasurer was standing at the king's side, and he replied for them. "Ceuta, Your Majesty. Ceuta in North Africa."

"Ceuta?"

"Yea, Ceuta. It is the most flourishing city in Mauretania [Morocco and part of Algeria]. With a fleet you could easily take it, and your sons could win knighthood with honor."

He went on to describe the city. It was on the African coast just opposite Gibraltar, and strategically it was of immense importance: shaped like a long thin thumb and dominated by a lofty hill, it had a secure harbor, from which the Moors who held it sent forth fusta after fusta (a fusta was a swift corsair ship) to dominate the passage from the Mediterranean to the Atlantic and to prey on Christian merchant vessels.

"You will have the praise of every Christian nation if you take it," said the treasurer, "for its slave marts and its harems are glutted with the men and women its vessels have taken. Slaves are as cheap as sparrows in Ceuta."

But Ceuta was worth taking for itself, he continued.

Founded in A.D. 534 by the great Byzantine emperor, Justinian, and originally called Septem Frates (the Seven Brothers) because of its seven hills, Ceuta had a magnificent trade, in the whole Mediterranean surpassed only by that of Venice and Alexandria. Ceuta commanded a rich tunny fishing area. And despite its nearness to the desert, it was surrounded by a fertile crescent where there were clear springs, acres of sugar cane, and groves of lime and orange trees.

João scratched his chin. "First I must know more about it, and not just the wealth I can find there," he said. "I must know about the height and thickness of the walls; the nature of its towers and turrets; what the prevailing winds are; whether its beaches are defended or undefended; and if they are defended, whether enough depth is carried close to the shore so that we can fight from the decks of our ships."

"Then find out," said Henry. "Send those who can inform you as to the place."

That would not be easy to do, however, for Christian ships were not usually permitted to anchor at Ceuta. Then João thought of a subterfuge. The widow of King Martin I of Sicily had asked for the hand of Duarte. He would send a mission to offer her Pedro's hand instead. Under the protocols of diplomacy, they would be able to touch at Ceuta both coming and going.

Thereupon he chose two of his most trusted councilors—Captain Affonso Furtado and Alvares Gonçalves Camelo, the prior of the Order of St. John. Off they went in two fine galleys.

But when they returned, they spoke little but nonsense.

"I visited Ceuta once before," said Captain Furtado, "when I was a small boy and my father was sent there as an ambassador. While I was there, I talked to an old man who told me that before he died, Portugal would have a king who would first defeat Castile and then destroy the Moors in Africa.

"The king was you," the captain continued, "and this prophecy means that you will conquer Ceuta. And you should, for there you will find everything as you wish it to be. Beaches and anchorages and everything."

But the prior made even less sense, the king thought, than Furtado did.

"Sire," he said. "I, too, looked carefully and observed, but I will not tell you anything unless you give me four things I need to do this." He named them: two bags full of sand, a reel of ribbon, a half bushel of beans, and a basin.

"I deal with two fools!" cried João. "I deal with two fools! For, look you, I ask them to report what they have seen, and one talks like an astrologer, and the other like a sorcerer."

Nevertheless, he gave the prior the materials he had asked for, and the latter then locked himself into a room. There he set to work. With the sand, he made a relief map of Ceuta and the hills behind it. He used the ribbon to show the walls and the beans for houses. He showed where the beaches were and he showed the citadel. He even showed Algeciras and Gibraltar and the Spanish coast across the strait.

Then he summoned the king and the princes. "Now put to me any questions you wish to. I will try to answer them." But there was no need to ask questions, for the sand, the beans, the ribbon, and the basin made everything plain.

João looked, and then capitulated. "It is decided," he told his sons. "We will go to Ceuta. That is, if your mother and Nun'Álvares approve." For he knew well that the Portuguese, love him as they did, would never follow him if either Philippa or the great constable refused to give their blessing.

The queen gave it eagerly. "No mother," she said, "wishes her sons to go on perilous missions, but these are not ordinary sons. They have come from a long line of emperors, kings, and princes who have won glory with their valor. I would not deny them the same opportunity."

Nun'Álvares approved too.

"In my opinion," was his verdict, "the idea did not come from any mortal. It came from God himself. It is a sin to oppose what God proposes."

Forthwith the preparations began. They continued for a full two years.

"The dockyards throughout the land were beautiful," said Azurara, who was a boy of thirteen or fourteen at the time. "They were filled with ships of every size and rig." Some of these came to be repaired and others to have their ribs strengthened so that they could support the shock of discharging cannon. But in the larger ports ships were built too. Indeed, every carpenter and caulker in the realm was pressed into service, and tree after tree was cut down to provide timber. In the smaller ports, the fishermen and their wives worked day and night gutting *bacalhau* (cod) and other fish, and then placing them to dry on hastily constructed flakes. Nor were they the only ones to toil until long after the sun had set. Throughout the kingdom, the beef butchers and the pork butchers, the cooks with their great caldrons, the coopers with their casks, and the makers of every kind of weapon worked day and night too.

No place was more active than Oporto, where Henry was in charge. Every road that led to it was jammed with ox wagons and mule trains laden with provisions and with lowing cattle shuffling and stumbling toward the slaughterhouse. There they would be butchered without delay and the meat stored in barrels. All the meat. The Portuenses (the inhabitants of Oporto) saved none for themselves.

"For the love of king and country," they cried, "we have become *tripeiros* (tripe eaters)!" They have been known as *tripeiros* ever since.

Men had to be provided too—men and the money to pay

them with—and in this matter João proceeded as cautiously as he had when he sent his spies to Ceuta. He summoned his treasurer into his presence. "We have adopted your plan," he told him, "and now you must make it possible for us to carry it out. Set your mints to coining money and yourself to devising new taxes."

João also directed his admiral, Mice Carlos, to begin assembling seamen while he himself caused a secret census to be taken. He wanted to know how many brave fellows would be available for his army.

Only when all this had been done and his preparations were more than half completed, did João at least partly come into the open. He convened a royal council at Torres Vedras, and swearing its members to absolute secrecy, told them what he proposed to do. There was a gasp of amazement followed by a pained silence. Then Nun'Álvares arose, followed by Duarte. Each said that he would follow the king. That was all that was needed. Councilor after councilor leaped to his feet and cried that he would do the same. The last one to speak was João Gomes de Silva, famous for his prowess and valor. Noting that, like him, all were veterans of old wars, he cried: "I am with you, Senhor! And what else can I say but 'Forward to the fray, graybeards!'" The councilors cheered and laughed.

The graybeards did indeed come forward, including one Ayres Gonçalves de Figuerido, who was ninety years old. Followed by a retinue of squires and foot soldiers, and wearing a battle-scarred coat of mail, he rode from his castle on a steed that looked as ancient as he did, and proclaimed that although age may have taken some of the strength from his arms, his spirit was as strong as ever.

But the young champions and would-be champions responded too. And not only Portuguese. Foreigners flocked in from half of Europe. A Londoner, Mundy, arrived. He brought with him four ships and a little company of men-at-arms and archers. Another Englishman, Iniquixius Dama (at least that was how the Portuguese recorded it), followed close behind. Antoine de La Salle, a French writer and knight, appeared too. Antoine was accompanied by two Picard knights, a Norman knight, and a German baron. It was even said that a German grand duke planned to join the expedition, but held back because no one could tell him where it was going. But so great was the love of adventure in those days that he was the only one to raise this objection, and he was told that if that was the way he felt, they could get along without him.

"Only the king and his council know," he was told, "and that will have to be enough for you."

The grand duke rode off in a huff.

At last everything was in readiness, and in June, 1415— June was an ideal month because the Atlantic gales are rare then—a royal messenger rode to Oporto. He bore the king's command to Henry.

"Set sail with all your ships for the mouth of the Tagus. There you will be met by Pedro."

This Henry did. Seventy ships in all, bright in their new paint and flying his blue, white, and black standard embroidered with his motto *talent de bien faire* ("desire to do well"), his fleet moved down the Portuguese coast, carried along by a balmy, early summer breeze. Finally, they reached the Tagus and, to the sound of trumpets, crossed the narrow bar. As promised, Pedro, with King João's even larger fleet, awaited them.

The two brothers waved to each other across the water, and brought their ships to anchor off Restello. Then they disembarked and rode to a nearby royal palace of Odivelas. There they found King João and Duarte.

"You have done well," João told Henry. "You have done

more than well. You have exceeded what should be expected
from one of your age."

Duarte echoed his father's words and added that he had a
personal reason to be pleased. "I have been told," he said,
"that I can leave my account books and my courts of justice
to go with you."

Always as modest as he was conscientious, Duarte had
thought that he would be left behind to manage the day by
day affairs of the kingdom during his father's absence as
leader of the expedition—and this although he had been as
eager as his brothers to win knighthood in battle.

But hardly had Duarte said this when one of his mother's
attendants entered the room. His face spoke tragedy.

"You know that the queen has been ill," he said, "but now
she is very ill. We fear that she is dying."

"Then we must call off the expedition!" cried João, and
he sent for a secretary to write the necessary orders.

Philippa, however, was not the kind of woman to permit
this. Instead, she summoned her sons to her sickbed and gave
each one of them a sword. "Use yours," she told Duarte, "as
a sword of justice." She turned to Pedro: "Use yours in defense
of the ladies." Finally, she came to Henry.

"Use yours to defend the nobly born of the land—the lords,
the knights, the gentlemen, the squires. They will not need
your help while your father reigns—or Duarte. But there will
be other kings in Portugal."

A wind rustled the curtains of her bedchamber.

"What wind is that?" she asked her husband. "Where does
it blow from?"

"It is a wind from the north," he told her.

"Then it is a good wind for your voyage. Do not delay. Sail
with it. My illness must not prevent your high adventure.
Sail with it before the feast day of St. James."

The feast day of St. James was July 25—less than a week

away. The Queen died the night after this conversation took place (either July 20 or July 21), and because it was feared that she had died of the plague, she was buried secretly before morning.

Then João turned to his three sons. "When can you be ready?" he asked.

"Whenever you say," said Henry. "The only delay will be the time it takes to weigh our anchors and to set our sails." The other two nodded in agreement.

"Then we will sail on Wednesday." Wednesday was July 24! "And not wearing mourning. Your mother and my wife would not wish it. She knows that feats of arms do not comport with tears and grieving. And she is now praying for us in heaven."

Sail they did—sixty-three transports, twenty-three triremes, thirty-two biremes, and one hundred twenty other ships (two hundred thirty-eight vessels in all) with twenty thousand men-at-arms and thirty thousand seamen aboard.

"It was a marvelous sight to see," says Azurara. "In the morning, the fleet was like a forest which had shed all its flowers and bore no more fruit. But then suddenly it became a glorious orchard, for the standards and the banners were of many forms and colors and they were unnumbered." So too were the swelling sails.

In the beginning, progress was swift and uneventful. Blown by Queen Philippa's wind, they rounded Cape St. Vincent on July 27, and that night anchored off Lagos. Lagos was an active seaport several miles to the east. There the purpose of the expedition was proclaimed by the royal chaplain, Fra João Xira. Obviously, they were not carrying Princess Isabella to England for a royal marriage or making war on Count William of Holland. (Rumors to this effect had been allowed to circulate.) But neither were they taking Pedro to the Queen of

Sicily, nor going to help the Pope of Rome against the Pope of Avignon (in those days there were two popes, and sometimes three popes), nor carrying crusaders to the Holy Land. Instead, they themselves were going to attack the infidel in his North African stronghold, and absolution was promised to all who took part in the attack. Absolution and booty. From fifty thousand throats, there came a cheer.

But at Faro near the border of Spain (a point reached on July 30) their troubles began. They were becalmed for a week while the pitch bubbled in the seams and the midsummer heat and the unfamiliar salt food drove the men almost mad with thirst. Then plague broke out on Henry's ship and fire on Duarte's. Duarte's hands were burned badly as he threw overboard the lantern which caused it. Finally, at Gibraltar, the Portuguese encountered a dense white fog which stretched from coast to coast, and through it, all but the smallest ships (these could anchor near shore) were carried toward Málaga by a strong eastward-flowing current. On top of this, a howling levanter (east wind) then struck the vessels and drove them back to their starting place. King João had planned to attack Ceuta at dawn on August 12. His fleet did not even anchor under its walls until August 27.

Although the levanter was an ill wind, it brought the Portuguese more than a little good. Indeed, without it their venture might not have succeeded. The ruler of Ceuta was a tough and wily Moor, Salah ben Salah, and even before the mission's purpose had been proclaimed at Lagos, he had rightly guessed that his city was its destination. Immediately he sent for aid to the King of Fez, who was the most powerful monarch in Morocco, and to the wild Berber tribesmen who lived in the nearby Atlas Mountains.

But when the ships were sighted in the offing only to disappear again, Salah changed his mind. The Portuguese were not going to attack Ceuta. Their goal was Gibraltar or Málaga or Cartagena.

"In that case," he told himself, "I no longer need allies."

Moreover allies not only were expensive but could be dangerous. If the King of Fez saved Ceuta, for example, he might make it his vassal and the raid-loving Berbers, even though they came as friends, might act like enemies. He dismissed them with thanks and they rode off.

But now the Portuguese were back again. What should he do?

He tried trickery first.

"As soon as the Moors in the city saw the fleet so near at hand," says Azurara, "they placed lights in all their windows. This was to make the Christians believe that the defenders were more numerous than they really were. Because the city was so large, it was a beautiful sight."

But trickery was not all that Salah relied on. The young Moors of the city were eager for battle, crying out that Allah would give them victory over the unbelievers.

"Their beautiful ships," they told Salah, "will end up in our shipyards. Their gold and silver chalices will be used at the weddings of our children. The rich ornaments of their chapels will decorate our mosques." They reasoned that they would meet the enemy on the beach, and there, since "the most of them and the best of them wear heavy steel armor," the invaders would bog down in the sand. "There, being light-armed, we will slay them like cattle."

Salah marshaled the young Moors along the shore.

The Portuguese were equally confident. Their ships were lighted up, too. Torchlight and lantern light shone on every deck and gleamed through every porthole as they went about their final tasks.

"O thou good sword of mine," cried one captain as he polished its blade, "how often hast thou, when God willed it, cut through mail and armor! We will see now if thou canst cut through the bare flesh of these paynims!"

"Pry open the casks," cried a second, "and let us eat the finest food, for this may be the last day of our lives! And, if by God's grace we live as victors, we will not need ship's food longer. There will be better food in Moorish larders!"

Others, however, sought their priests to confess their sins. Only when it was well past midnight did they retire to their bunks.

The attack began at dawn. Henry was not the first to land. He had been promised this honor, but as he paused to receive his chaplain's blessing, a subordinate leaped from the gangplank ahead of him. However, the young prince with one hundred and fifty followers was not far behind.

His first objective was the great Almina Gate—Ceuta's principle one—and to win to it, he and his men had to fight their way through the young Moors Salah had placed on the beach.

The latter were led by a huge and naked warrior.

"He was black as a crow," reported an eyewitness, "with long white teeth and thick full lips. He hurled rocks with the force of a catapult." Only when he was slain by one of Henry's retainers could the Portuguese advance, but then they poured into the city. Once in it, some of them halted to catch their breath—the battle had already raged for five hours and its noise was so great that it could be heard in Algeciras, fifteen miles distant across the straits—but Henry, his sword drawn, and with only seventeen followers, pressed on through the narrow and winding streets toward the triple-walled citadel. This was where the Moors made their last stand.

He was all day in winning to it, and so savage was the fighting that only four of his men survived it; in fact a message was even brought to João saying that Henry had been slain too. "A soldier must expect this," was his only comment.

Then suddenly, as a thin new moon shone silvery against

the sky's blue velvet, there was no resistance from the huge citadel. Birds roosted peacefully in the crannies of the walls from which missiles had been hurled only a little earlier. Henry entered the fortress only to find it deserted except for one Basque and one Italian, who were prisoners there. Salah ben Salah and his fighting men had fled.

They were not pursued. The rough Portuguese soldiers and sailors and the five hundred Christian slaves they had liberated had other things to occupy them. In the fifteenth century, it was the accepted right of a victorious army to pillage any city it conquered, and at Ceuta the victors systematically set about doing this. They burst into beautiful tiled rooms to lay hands on carved or inlaid tables and chairs, priceless Eastern embroidery, Indian muslin, and Persian carpets. They smashed into and looted warehouses, ripping bags of precious spices in their haste and thus filling the streets with pungent scent. They dug up gardens, looking for chests filled with gold, and lowered men into wells, hoping to find jewels or silver. Even the poorest-looking Moor who fell into their hands was tortured. Perhaps he could reveal the whereabouts of something of value they had not found.

It was only after a night of this that João proclaimed Ceuta a Christian city (it still is a Christian city) under his protection. He ordered its great mosque to be consecrated as a Christian cathedral. It was purified with salt and water, and in it were hung two beautiful bronze bells which Moorish pirates had carried off from Lagos twenty years earlier and were now part of the booty taken by the Portuguese. Then a high mass was celebrated and a *Te Deum* sung as word was sent to the Pope that the first church in Africa had been taken from the Moslems and restored to Christian hands.

This done, King João thought of his sons. He would knight them in the very place where they had earned knighthood.

"Henry first," he said. But Henry would not permit this.

"Let us be knighted in the order of our ages. This would be more fitting."

João complied, and then bestowed further honors upon them.

"Since he is my first-born and my heir, I can do little for Duarte. But let him take for his own such of my lands as he wishes, and in my lifetime. As for you, Pedro, I will make you Duke of Coimbra, and you Henry, I will make Duke of Viseu."

He also made Henry Lord of Covilhã, a title which would bring him revenues as well as honor.

"This is because," João said, "of his greater perils at Ceuta."

Then he, his three sons, and the greater part of his army embarked on the flag-bedecked ships to return triumphantly to Portugal. He left behind only a small handful of men, commanded by one of his captains, Dom Pedro de Menezes. "I do not need more men, for I can defend Ceuta with a hockey stick," Dom Pedro told João, and events would prove him right.

Thus the three princes had won the knighthood they longed for, and with it honor and glory, but what lay ahead of them now that they had done this? They were still young men. Even Duarte, the eldest, was only twenty-four. What would they do in the days and years to come?

With Duarte, there was no problem. He would go back to the dull business of learning the art of kingship, and, if he had any time left over, read and write and occasionally ride. Pedro would begin his longed-for travels. But what about Henry, the ablest, if the youngest, of the three brothers? What would be a fit occupation for him?

João vetoed an attack upon another infidel city and particularly an attack upon Gibraltar. Castile harbored designs of one day capturing that Moslem stronghold, and João did not want to antagonize Castile—and perhaps start a new war with her. And Henry's help was not needed at Ceuta. Dom Pedro de Menezes successfully repulsed Salah ben Salah's attempt to retake Ceuta, although this time Salah was aided by both the King of Fez and the King of Granada, who sent his nephew with a large army.

Another possibility was for Henry to seek service with a foreign lord. He received many invitations to do this. Pope Martin V urged him to take command of one of the contingents he was sending against the Hussites of Bohemia (now Czechoslovakia). The Hussites were religious reformers led by John Huss. If that did not suit Henry, the Pope said, he could ride eastward and help the Byzantine emperor, Manuel II, defend Constantinople against the Turks. His cousin, Henry V of England, who had just won the battle of Agincourt, asked him to ride at his side and help him take Paris. Even Juan II of Castile solicited his aid. Juan still looked suspiciously at Portugal, but he would have been grateful to have Henry fight with him in the wars he was continually waging with neighboring Aragon.

Henry refused them one and all. "I am a Portuguese and I would only serve Portugal," he said.

And then he knew how he could do this. The seed of the idea had been sown at Ceuta.

"Inland from that city," he had been told, "there is a wide sea of sand which separates the whites from the blacks." This was the Sahara Desert. "But the Carthaginians [today we call them the Tunisians] travel across it. They travel in caravans of seven hundred camels for the sake of the gold that is found beyond it. But the trip is dangerous and it often happens that only one tenth of the people and animals manage to return."

If the trip was worth making, surely there must be a better way of making it. There was. And Henry jumped from his sleep—his friend Azurara says he literally did do this—and cried he knew the answer. "Why not," he said, "send expeditions over the paths of the sea to reach this gold?" And not only the gold and the mysterious gold kingdoms, but beyond them the realm of Prester John and even India.

All he needed was a base of operations. He went to his father. "Sire," he said on bended knee, "make me the governor of the Algarve." The Algarve is the southermost province of Portugal. It is bounded on the east by Spain and on the west and south by the Atlantic Ocean. Henry's interest was not in the whole of the Algarve, just in a particular place: a peninsula about three miles southeast of Cape St. Vincent. It is three quarters of a mile long and nowhere more than four hundred yards wide. At its narrowest point, it is about two hundred yards wide. Its jagged gray cliffs fall directly into the sea one hundred and eighteen feet below, and this sea surges night and day against them, throwing up great noisy columns of spray that make the whole shore line look like a gam of whales blowing. Being on it is like standing upon the wind-swept deck of a ship.

The peninsula has always been surrounded with an air of mystery. In ancient days, white-robed Druids had a place of worship there and for that reason it became known as the *Promontorium Sacrum* (Sacred Cape). The Greek geographers said that it was there the land ended and the ocean began. Wise men who reached it, they said, would go no farther. The Arabs had named it *Charak Rach* (Isle of the Rocks) but gradually it became known as Sagrom, and then Sagres. With Cape St. Vincent, it was the southwesternmost point of Europe and the nearest by water to the places of which Henry dreamed. And there would be no distractions there.

"The Algarve?" said João to his son. "You wish to be its governor? I appoint you this—and in perpetuity."

"I thank you, Sire," said Henry. "And I will depart forth-with."

Indeed, he was so eager to be on his way that he did not wait to organize a fitting escort but set out almost immediately with a single companion. Across the Tagus he went and then on through the rugged southern province of Alentejo with its forests of cork oak and holm oak, and its mile after mile of heath and cistus. Presently the air grew balmier and the vegetation more tropical. Now there were dates, palms, aloes, and cacti. After not too many days, he reached the little hamlet of Raposeira. This was nothing but a collection of hovels but it was only a mile and a half inland from Henry's destination. There, in one of those hovels, he took up his residence. He would stay there—when he was not at Lagos, that is—until a place of his own had been made ready.

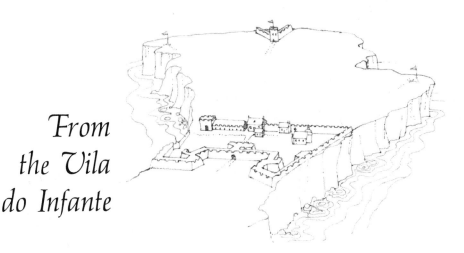

From the Vila do Infante

Although this establishment took years to complete, work almost certainly began at once (around 1418), and hardly had Henry arrived in the Algarve when the terns, herring gulls, oyster catchers, and stilts which inhabited the lonely shore were disturbed by the hustle and bustle of arriving workmen.

The first need was for a seaport and a shipyard. For miles around, the exposed and rock-strewn coast offered little shelter. Even at Lagos, landing is still described as "at all times difficult and sometimes dangerous." The ships which passed by as they sailed from the Atlantic to the Mediterranean or vice versa, were, as Henry put it, "without the comfort of provisions and with hardly any water." Worse than that, if they were shipwrecked and their sailors cast upon the beach, there was no place to bury them.

The navigator, said a friend, was "moved with pity" by the plight of these seafarers. And, too, he wanted "the merchants and all those who pass from East to West" to pause, come ashore, and talk to him. What better way to entice them than to provide them with all they needed—from a safe anchorage to supplies and repairs?

Tercenanabal (naval arsenal)—only later was it known as Vila do Infante, or Prince Royal's Town—did just that, and so well was it planned and situated that even before it was finished, Genoa offered to buy it. She wanted to add it to the string of trading stations she was setting up from North Africa to the Black Sea.

"At a great price!" says Azurara.

Henry refused them indignantly. "All they want to do is make money!" he cried.

Although he permitted his captains to make money—remember, he was first inspired by the caravans that brought gold to Ceuta—and although he accepted his share of it, his interest was in something else. It was in the promotion of exploration for its own sake, and for the sake of learning all he could of those lands "about which there was no knowledge either in writing or in the memory of man."

"Something hidden. Go and find it!" says a mysterious whisper to the hero of Rudyard Kipling's poem, "The Explorer." Henry would say the same to those who sailed his ships for him. He would add: "And when you have found it, come back and tell me about it. In detail."

Tercenanabal—the shipyard and arsenal—was, however, only the first step. As year followed year—and when Azurara wrote his chronicle forty years later, the hammering was still going on—thick walls arose, and building after building was constructed: the little white seaman's chapel of Nossa Senhora da Rocha (Our Lady of the Rock); the Church of St. Catherine, and adjoining it the cemetery; a hospital; a few warehouses; a dwelling or two for such weather-beaten seafarers as wanted a brief respite from crowded and often foul-smelling quarters on shipboard; Prince Henry's court—or palace, if you could call it that—and his study; an observatory, the first in Portugal; a fort to protect the palace; and also—but mainly at Raposeira and Lagos—numerous inns and lodging houses, to provide accommodations for all the many people Henry hoped and believed would be drawn to him once his purpose became widely known.

These hopes and this belief were more than fulfilled. In a small trickle at first but then in a swelling flood, men came to him from "such a variety of nations with customs so unlike our own," that, said a foreign visitor, "it was a marvel and an education to see them and listen to them." Genoese, Venetians, and Catalans. (Barcelona, the largest Catalan city, was a major seaport in the Middle Ages, and the so-called sea law of Barcelona is a model for some of the maritime law that is still in force.) Englishmen, Frenchmen, Germans, and Scandanavians. Arabs and Jews and Moors. (Although Henry was intensely religious, he did not share the religious prejudices of the day.) There was even a man referred to only as "the Indian Jacob." Some think that Jacob was not an Indian at all. They contend that he was an Ethiopian. Either is entirely possible. Azurara says specifically that *both* Indians and Ethiopians came to Sagres, and that Henry gave them gifts. They came, he says "to see the beauty of the world."

If they were of all nations, the men who came to Sagres were also of every profession. Many were scholars, especially those who studied the earth and the heavens above it, such as geographers, mapmakers, astronomers, astrologers, cosmographers, mathematicians (they would help Henry calculate positions and distances from the observations made by his captains), and students of nature. But there were also master mariners, world travelers, and every kind of captain of fortune and adventurer.

One of the most important of the men of learning was

Jahuda Cresques of Mallorca who after his baptism—he was born a Jew—was known to the Portuguese as Mestre (Master) Jácome.

Mestre Jácome was the distinguished son of a distinguished father. Abraham Cresques, *magister mappamundorum et buxolorum* (master of world maps and compasses), taught at Mallorca's renowned school of navigation. He was also the designer of the Catalan Atlas, one of the best of medieval atlases; a manufacturer of navigational instruments; and the perfecter of a series of tables by which one could calculate the distance traveled at sea.

When Abraham died, he left all his papers to Jácome, and Henry at once sent an emissary to the latter. "Come to Sagres and you will be paid a princely salary," he was told. The youthful scholar came.

But Mestre Jácome was not the only distinguished member of the band of men who gathered around Henry and offered him their help. The mathematics professor, Fra Egidio of Bologna, could aid Henry when he had calculations to make—and that was often. Patrizio de' Conti, son of the Niccolo Conti who a generation earlier had traveled as far east as India, had talked long and often with his father. He maintained that all the tales told by men like William de Rubruquis and Marco Polo were true. (Dom Pedro had brought Henry a rare manuscript of Marco's *Travels* and Henry poured over it night and day.) There *was* a gorgeous East, Conti said, and it was fabulous! Juan de Morales, a Spanish pilot who had spent years of captivity in North Africa, repeated to Henry the stories of Africa and the Atlantic which he had heard from his captors. The charts of Mestre Pedro, a second maker of maps and figures, were especially treasured because he illuminated them in color and illustrated them with pictures.

Perhaps it was the tough sea dogs and adventurers who

made the biggest contribution to Henry's being able to realize his purposes, for it was they who drew the men of learning to the so-called School of Sagres.

The Vila do Infante was not really a school as we think of a school today. It was instead a congenial meeting place where men who were interested in the same things Henry was could listen and talk—and be well rewarded for doing this, since, as Azurara says, "nobody ever went away from the prince with empty hands."

They soon had plenty to talk about, for at Henry's orders, out went *barca* after *barca*, and *barinel* after *barinel*, not only from Lagos and Sagres but from almost every other Portuguese seaport. (A *barca* was a relatively small vessel of less than twenty-five tons. Short, stubby, and half-decked, it had a mainmast with a single square sail as well as a mizzen, which was not always used. A *barinel* was larger—its tonnage could be as much as fifty—and carried the same sails and spars, but it had oars in addition.)

Into the distance they sailed, and then after weeks or even months, they came back again. The first thing their captains did was report to Henry. They reported no wild tales of men who were half-monster or of scaly sea beasts as sailors had done in the days of yore, but rather matters of practical importance to all who sailed. Here there are good harbors, or there are no good harbors. There the bottom is sandy and the holding ground is excellent. It is the only good holding ground for many leagues. In such and such a place, there are bars and shoals. They are dangerous during a gale, but they can be crossed in calm weather. Along this coast, returning vessels will encounter head winds and an adverse current. There, the tides are of so many fathoms or feet. This was the compass course, and the land we came to is so many miles (or day's journey) distant. Here is what we found.

Madeira was the first discovery—or maybe *rediscovery* would be a better word. For over and above the fact that it may have been known to the Greeks and the Romans and perhaps the Arabs, most fourteenth-century maps are strewn with real or imaginary islands, and Madeira may be one of them. According to Brito Ribello, a Portuguese historian, it was visited during the reign of Henry's uncle, Fernando I (1367–1383), by one Machico, "a master of his own ship," who wandered there accidentally.

It was also supposed to have been discovered at about the same time by an Englishman, Robert Machin, and an English-woman, Anne d'Arfet. This was one of the stories Juan de Morales had heard during his captivity and told to Henry.

Robert, it goes, was a handsome squire and Anne the daughter of a lord; they lost their hearts to each other and wished to marry, but her father would not allow them to. Worse than that, he imprisoned Robert and married Anne to another man. But love found a way. Robert was released, Anne fled from her husband, and together they made their way to Bristol, where they set sail for France. They never got there. Instead they were blown for thirteen days before a northeast gale to the shores of an uninhabited island. There Anne died of exposure and two days later, Robert died of heartbreak.

"The survivors," said Morales, "made a small boat and in it reached Morocco. One of them shared a cell with me. Anne and Robert, he said, were buried under a great tree and their epitaph was carved on it. The island was Madeira."

It is doubtful that Henry heard Machico's story and he did not learn of Robert and Anne until his own ships were sailing far and wide, so for all practical purposes Madeira remained an undiscovered island until 1419 or 1420. Then two of Henry's young servitors, João Gonçalves Zarco (Zarco means "blue-eyed") and Tristão Vaz Terceira, set forth toward the coast of Africa, only to be driven far out to sea by a violent storm. Buffeted by huge waves, their vessel almost foundered, but then the gales ceased and the skies grew fair. Before them lay a small island with a white sandy beach off which there was good anchorage. They named it Porto Santo (Holy Haven) in gratitude, and hastened back to Henry. (Porto Santo— it still has this name—was not Madeira, but an island near it.)

"It is a new land," they told him. "It is not one of the Canaries. Its soil is rich too. It could be colonized."

"Then do so and forthwith," commanded Henry.

Back went Zarco and Tristão Vaz with men and seeds. They were accompanied by Bartholomeu Perestrello, who one day would be Christopher Columbus's father-in-law. Perestrello brought with him a single doe rabbit, which he released. Then the troubles began. Crops grew, but the rabbits multiplied and ate everything. After two years, the colonists gave up in discouragement and went back to Portugal.

Henry summoned Zarco and Tristão Vaz and together they related to him the unhappy story. "And yet," said Zarco, "and yet, there was one thing—"

"What one thing?" Henry broke in.

"Always on the horizon there was a low black cloud which never moved. What it was, we do not know."

"And you did not seek to find out?"

"No, *Infante.*"

"Go back at once and bring me the answer!"

Thus commanded, Zarco and Tristão Vaz put to sea for the third time. They reached Porto Santo late in June 1425, paused there for a few days, and toward dusk on July 1, weighed anchor and sailed toward the mysterious shadow. At dawn, they were close to it. Ahead of them they heard a low moaning, and saw a line of white.

"Turn back!" the sailors cried. "The sea is boiling."

"Fools!" cried Zarco and Tristão Vaz. "It is nothing but the surf breaking—and on another shore."

They were right. The sun rose, and as it did, the fog lifted and there before their eyes was one of the loveliest islands they had ever seen. Tall mountains—the tallest, Pico Ruivo, is six thousand feet high—huge and luxuriant forests, in which grew not only pine but every kind of hardwood, flowers of every color, even a half a dozen splashing streams.

This was Madeira, and it was a real place for colonists. Henry, who immediately divided the land between its two discoverers, forthwith sent out shipload after shipload of them. (One of these colonists was so convinced that Madeira was another Garden of Eden that he named his two children, the first born on the island, Adam and Eve.) They set up the first permanent colony (the first colony to last right up to the present) ever to be established by Europeans outside of Europe. It was a real paradise. Everything prospered there, and with its lace, its linen, its world-famous wine, and its climate, to some extent everything still does.

The Azores were discovered—or rediscovered—early too, and in their case, just as in the case of Madeira, there is some doubt as to when and by whom. Some authorities insist that the 1341 voyage described by Boccaccio went to the Azores rather than to the Canaries, and several historians say that the islands were shown on a Florentine map drawn as early as 1351.

But if Europeans had reached the Azores at that early date, they, like Madeira, were shortly forgotten, and their true discoverer was one of Henry's captains, Gonçalo Velho Cabral. He was sent out in either 1427 or 1432 with instructions "to see if you can find any of the islands which I believe there must be in the western ocean."

He found only a half-mile-long line of black rocks—the highest, Hormigon, rises but thirty-five feet above sea level—

and promptly named them Las Formigas (The Ants). He then returned to Henry, not realizing that he was only twenty miles from his goal.

"They are the only land there is," he reported, "and little good will they do you since the surf rolls completely over them in stormy weather."

"But there must be other land," said Henry, "for they could not rise all by themselves from the deep ocean. There must be other land. Go back and find it."

Velho obeyed and at dawn on August 15 sighted the twin peaks of a true island. This really was one of the Azores. He named it Santa Maria because he had found it on the day of the Assumption of the Virgin Mary, but in his lifetime it was always known as Gonçalo Velho's island.

"It is no Madeira," he informed his prince, "but beeches and cedars grow on it and there is a fragrant undergrowth of juniper and laurel and heath. It is fertile and well watered too, and there is ample pasture land."

"I will make you captain of it," said Henry. "That is, if you will settle it."

This seemed a fair offer, and Velho accepted. Out went livestock, building material, farmers—and fishermen. The waters around Santa Maria teemed with tuna, mullet, and bonito, and offshore, one could see porpoises, dolphins, and whales.

Not too long afterward, another island of the Azores was discovered, São Miguel, and again by Gonçalo Velho. The story is that an escaped slave climbed to the summit of Santa Maria's tallest peak and dimly in the distance saw tall peaks. Hoping to be rewarded with his freedom, he told his master, who told Velho. After that, the Azores were discovered one after another. Terceira (the "third" island), Graciosa, Pico, São Jorge, and Fayal. (Only Corvo and Flores were not discovered until late in Henry's lifetime.)

At this time, the group was given its name: the Azores, or

Hawk Islands. *Açor* is the Portuguese word for hawk, and Henry's sailors thought they saw many hawks there; what they probably saw were sea gulls.

Not all the islands were settled immediately, to be sure. On some of them the Portuguese merely put ashore cattle, sheep, goats, and poultry, so that shipwrecked mariners would have something to live on. It was a common custom in those days. The devils heard by Sir George Somers and his crew when they were cast ashore on Bermuda were actually swine left by Spanish seafarers. Nevertheless, Portugal had now established a second outpost in the Atlantic Ocean. It would be very useful to her in the years to come.

But even as Henry's captains sailed out beyond the western horizon, Henry's hopes and dreams lay elsewhere. He had never forgotten the gold caravans he had seen at Ceuta. It was the coast of Africa he wished his vessels to explore, and in particular he wanted them to round Cape Bojador (Cape Bulgy), which thrusts out from the continent about one hundred miles south of the Canaries.

As described today in the United States Hydrographic Office's *Sailing Directions* for that part of the world, the cape hardly deserves its name, for "the mass of red sand" of which it consists does not bulge into the sea more than many another African cape, and most of its supposedly frightening offshore reefs are in fact only "schools of sardines, having the appearance of reefs."

But in Henry's time it was regarded as an obstacle that barred all progress. In the belief of the day, you simply could not sail beyond it.

(Not too much earlier, Cape Noun [Cape Not], about one hundred miles north of the Canaries, was regarded as a similar obstacle. Either you did *not* sail beyond this point, said an old jingle, or you did *not* return. But Cape Noun had long since been passed.)

Needless to say, the Arabs did all they could to encourage the belief that Cape Bojador could not be passed. Why should they help the Christian Portuguese to outflank them and find a sea route to a trade which was so important to them? They revived the old fable that beyond Bojador the world ended in the Sea of Obscurity, and invented some new fables to go with it. But the Portuguese sailors did not need Arab stories to discourage them. They had only to look at the shore once they were south of the Atlas Mountains and see little but alternating bare bleak rocks and sand dunes over which the harmattan (a dry, dusty, parching desert wind) blew night and day. Not only was there no safe anchorage; there was no reason to anchor.

Henry understood these feelings. "No sailor or merchant would go there of his own free will," he admitted, "for such men only want to navigate where they know they can make a profit."

He, however, was neither a merchant nor a merchant's shipman. He summoned one of his squires, Gil Eannes.

"I am giving you a barca with a crew of fifteen men," he told him. "With it, sail past Bojador."

This was in 1433. Out went Gil—as far as northern West Africa and the Canaries, the latter inhabited since prehistoric days by a Stone Age people. In both places he seized merchandise and money from French and Castilian ships he found cruising there. He also landed and brought back natives whom he could sell as slaves. But as for Bojador and passing it— indeed not! For he now knew even more of its dangers than he had when he set out. Have no doubt of it, his Moorish and his Guanche (native Canarian) captives filled his ears with them. He had also talked with four Flemish captains who were engaged in the Canary trade and who, like the Arabs, wanted to frighten off competitors.

They succeeded in frightening Gil. Back to Henry he went,

crying that it was impossible to round Cape Bojador. "I know for I have talked to men who tried to."

This is one of the few times that Henry ever showed his anger.

"You, Gil Eannes, whom I brought up as a small boy!" he cried. "You to fail me! You to turn back! You to be frightened by the cock-and-bull stories told you by four shallow-water sailors who have never used a compass or a chart!"

But then his voice softened. "Come now, be sensible! All I ask you to do is round a little point of land, and you will be given honors and rewards!"

Gil shuffled his feet and bowed his head, abashed. "If you will allow me to, I will go again, and this time I will do what you asked me to do," he said.

"If I *allow* you?" said Henry. "I *command* you."

And so for the second time the little barca set forth, but now there was a determined jut to her captain's jaw.

The first part of the voyage was pleasant enough. The water was blue and sparkling, and although it was summer, the temperature was bearable. But as Gil approached the Moroccan coast, the heat grew greater every day until the pitch boiled in the seams and his men had to live in the shadow of the sails. To walk on the deck barefoot was an agony.

South of Cape Noun, the sea turned red, colored by Sahara sand washed down by a stream which rose in the Atlas Mountains. Then it turned bottle green, and as a south-flowing current hurried them onward, they could see Fuerteventura (one of the Canaries) looming like an enormous whale to starboard. Cape Juby, where the Vivaldi brothers had disappeared in 1291, was to port.

At last the promontory they sought! At last Cape Bojador! It was long and low and as they drew near it, they could see a white welter of waves around it and hear the sea beast moaning of the West African surf.

The crew panicked at this. "Turn back!" they cried. "Turn back, or we are lost!"

Gil Eannes humored them. "I will not turn back," he said, "but I will stand out to sea." And for a day and a half he did.

Then during the night he turned southward again, and after that eastward, until at dawn they saw before them a long stretch of land which ran on and on until it was lost in haze.

But it was not Cape Bojador! For without his men knowing it, Gil had rounded that formidable piece of land.

"Drop anchor!" he commanded as his ship bobbed up and down in front of a triangular patch of white sand. Then he had himself rowed ashore. There he found a desolate expanse where there was neither man nor beast nor even trees—only a few low-growing shrubs with small flowers on them.

He picked a handful and dried them carefully. This done, he started back to Portugal and there hastened to Prince Henry. He knelt before him.

"The dread cape is dread no more," he said, "for I have done what you bade me and have seen it astern of me. In proof, here are some flowers I plucked there. In Portugal, we call them St. Mary's roses."

Henry took them in one hand and pressed them to his lips. With the other, he lifted Gil to his feet, embracing him as he might have embraced a brother.

That was the beginning—but it was only the beginning. For even as Henry was listening to Gil Eannes's tale, his shipwrights and his shipyard workers were fitting out a barinel to make the same voyage. (Presumably he chose a barinel because it had oars and would not be completely dependent on fair winds and currents.) This he placed under the command of Affonso Gonçalves Baldaya, his cupbearer.

"You and Gil Eannes will go to Bojador again," he said, "and you will again sail past it. But this time you will explore the land more thoroughly."

They did. They not only reached Bojador, but continued for another one hundred and fifty miles until they came to a place which they called Angra de Ruivos, or Redfish Bay. They came back with tantalizing tidings.

"We saw more than flowers," they told Henry. "We saw the footprints of men and of camels."

"If there are footprints," said Henry, "then men and dwelling places cannot be distant. Go back and seek again."

This time, however, he sent only Baldaya—perhaps Gil Eannes wanted a rest from seafaring—but the cupbearer now knew the way and he not only reached Redfish Bay, but went on until he came to an estuary "almost like the mouth of a wide river." He promptly named it the Rio do Ouro (River of Gold). Although it was not a river but a bay, it is known as the Río de Oro (the Spanish version of Rio do Ouro) today.

Here, one hundred and twenty leagues beyond Cape Bojador, he anchored. (Today a league varies from 2.4 miles to 4.6 miles but since it is approximately two hundred miles from Bojador to the Río de Oro, either Henry's captains were inaccurate or his leagues shorter.) "Among other things," says Azurara, "Baldaya had brought two horses; he put these ashore and ordered two youths"—Hector Homem and Diogo Lopes—"to mount them and ride into the country looking carefully on every side for villages."

Hector and Diogo set out. They were armed only with their lances and swords and were equipped with neither body armor nor shields "since these would impede them if they had to flee." Following the shore of the bay, they rode for some twenty-one miles. Then they came upon a party of nineteen natives who "were without any arms of offense or defense, but only assagais."

"They did not stand," said Hector, "but fled to a little hill. There rocks protected them, and they held us off for the rest of the day. Then the sun began to set and we thought it wiser to retreat. Here we are."

Here they were, one of them slightly wounded in the foot, but soon they were back again, for after giving them a short repose, Baldaya put the two young men ashore once more, and bade them retrace their steps. He and a party of his men would follow in the ship's boat. But when they reached the place where the skirmish had taken place, the natives had vanished.

"They did leave behind their poor belongings," Baldaya told Henry later, "and these I took with me to show to you."

After that, Baldaya returned to the mouth of the estuary and there he found a great multitude of sea lions—it is said that they may have numbered five thousand. He had his men kill as many as they could and load the barinel with their skins.

But he was still unsatisfied, for he had not come all this way to bring back skins. So he went on for about a hundred and fifty miles to see, he said, if he could "make captive some man, woman, or child" to show to Henry. Here he came to a point shaped like a ship, and named it Punta Galha (Port of the Galley). He landed, and again found no men. But he did find finely woven nets made from the bark of a tree.

"They are as good as any made of linen in Spain or Portugal," he told Henry.

"Yet, at that," he continued, "my voyage was a failure, for you sent me to find out something about the men of the country. I now come back knowing that there are men—but we knew that when Gil Eannes and I journeyed together—but not knowing of what sort and whether they are Moors (Moslems) or Gentiles (regarded in those days as idol-worshiping savages). I do not know what their way of living is either."

Baldaya underestimated himself, however. It was only two years earlier that Gil Eannes had broken down medieval superstition by rounding Bojador, and already this second Portuguese captain had gone some five hundred and fifty miles beyond it. Henry could now confidently send captain after captain and ship after ship farther and farther down the coast of Africa.

Henry would have done just this, and perhaps reached his goal almost before he had begun seeking it, had he not been a king's son and then a king's brother. As such, he was drawn away from Sagres for a while and into the affairs of the kingdom, and to the one truly great failure—it also brought with it a devastating personal tragedy—of his long and successful life.

The Constant Prince

At the time of the rounding of Cape Bojador, King João was seventy-six and his health was failing rapidly. In the spring of 1433, his doctors ordered him to Alcochete on the banks of the Tagus, hoping that its rural surroundings would benefit him.

Instead, he grew weaker every day. Realizing that the end could not be far off, he ordered his sons to have him carried in a litter to Lisbon. "I do not want to die in the private house of some citizen!" he said. In Lisbon, on the fourteenth of August —it was the forty-eighth anniversary of the battle which gave him his throne—he breathed his last peacefully in the presence of his sons and his servitors.

"We, too, have lost a father!" cried his subjects.

They had. João was a great soldier, but he was more than that. He was a strong ruler who had wrested power from the nobility and given it to the merchants and the plain people. He was a wise ruler who had used the sword himself but in the kingdom replaced violence with law and order based on what was good for all. At his death even the lowliest peasant could feel safe.

Small wonder that the whole land went into spontaneous mourning! The royal catafalque—preceded by Duarte, Pedro, Henry, João, and Fernando, and by the knights and lords of the realm, who were clad in black but bore brightly colored banners—was drawn by five splendid horses the sixty miles between Lisbon and the great monastery of Batalha, where King João was to be buried. Along the road there was a shoulder-to-shoulder multitude.

It is even said that a miracle took place at João's funeral.

"During the ceremonies," wrote a monk, "the cathedral consumed six tapers and twenty-four torches, made up of two hundred and forty pounds of wax. But after the ceremonies were concluded, *two hundred and sixty-four and a half* pounds of wax were left." The wax had grown instead of shrinking!

The new king was another kind of man. João throve on action, but Duarte liked to brood. He was an intellectual in every sense of the word—one of the foremost royal intellectuals in a part of Europe which had already produced such learned kings as Alfonso the Wise of Castile and Duarte's own cultivated forebears, Sancho I and Diniz.

Duarte read copiously. He wrote too, and indeed some called him Duarte the Eloquent because he understood so well "the grammar and logic of his language." We know the titles of twenty-two of his works. They include treatises on riding, fencing, astronomy—and how to cast out devils.

He also wrote at least five or six works on how to govern. In these, he gave himself—and any other ruler who read them—all kinds of good advice. However, when it came to carrying out this advice, Duarte was apt to stumble. There were always two sides to every question and he usually vacillated between them.

His father understood this very well. "Cease your clerking and pay attention to common sense," he once told his son.

"*Res, non verba*—Deeds, not words!" Henry echoed.

But Duarte was like his famous ancestor, Richard Coeur de Lion, who changed his mind so often that he was known as Richard Yea-and-Nay. "Intelligence is our best virtue," he said once. And no one who was intelligent would act in haste.

Furthermore, Duarte did not want to be king and the coronation itself took place amid gloomy forebodings. At dawn that day, his confessor aroused him. "Wake up, Sire!" he cried. "Wake up to your royal duties!" But Duarte, instead of leaping from his bed, covered his face with his hands and began weeping.

When he did get up, he was halted by Mestre Guedelha, the court astrologer. Mestre Guedelha knelt before him.

"Postpone your putting on the crown, Sire!" he implored. "Postpone it at least until the afternoon! For there is danger, Sire! The stars have warned me! Jupiter is retrogressing. The sun is shadowed! The stars foretell disaster!"

"Would I could!" replied Duarte gloomily. "Would I could, and postpone it forever! But if I have faith in you, I have greater faith in God who is over all things."

"But I ask only that you postpone it a few hours—even an hour!"

"No!" cried Duarte. "No! I will not listen! God commands me, and I must not waver."

"Then you will reign but a few years," cried Mestre Guedelha, "and those filled with burdens and anxieties."

"I must do what God bids me, what it is my duty to do," was Duarte's response.

This said, he moved slowly to the palace gate. A cortege had formed there and he moved at its head toward the Terreiro do Paço (Palace Square) where the Bishop of Évora awaited him. Clad in pontificals, the latter preached a long sermon and then, when the royal banner had been unfurled, commanded silence.

"*Real! Real! Real!* [Royal! Royal! Royal!]" he shouted. "I give you Dom Duarte of Portugal, now our lord."

The applause reverberated.

Even this, however, did not lift Duarte's spirits. "Do you not think," he asked the bishop when they had returned to the palace, "that it were better had you burned a handful of tow before me as a reminder that the pomps and glories of the world are fleeting?"

"Since you know this," the bishop replied, "burning tow was not needed. Moreover, you are monarch now. Act and think like one."

Only then did the new king face up to reality. At this moment, says one of his biographers, he "squared his shoulders and faced the problems of his reign." Or at any rate, he tried to.

There were many problems and they began at once. First was the question of an almost empty treasury. On September 22, 1428, Duarte had married Leonora, daughter of the King of Aragon, amid ceremonies, reported Henry to his father, so long and exhausting that at their conclusion the bride fainted.

Dom Pedro was married the next year—also to a Spanish princess, the daughter of the Count of Urgel—and later in the year Duarte's only sister, Isabella, was betrothed to Philip the Good of Burgundy, who had been sent a portrait of her by Jan van Eyck and fallen in love with her.

The two weddings cost much, but the betrothal cost more. The dowry alone was 200,000 crowns, and in addition João had sponsored a series of magnificent jousts and tournaments and bestowed rich presents all around. Even the flutists and minstrels "who arrived on horseback and performed melodiously on trumpets and other instruments" were tossed bulging purses. He wanted to impress these rough but rich northerners.

As a result, when Duarte became king, his coffers were bare.

Castile was a problem, too. In those days, the Spanish

peninsula was divided into five kingdoms: Navarre in the north; Aragon in the northeast; Castile extending from the Bay of Biscay to Seville and bordering Portugal on the east; Portugal in the west; and in the south, Moorish Granada. These kingdoms were almost always at war with one another, particularly Castile and Portugal. This was because there was hardly a Castilian prince who did not claim to be King of Portugal, or vice versa.

But Aragon and Castile were at sword's point too, and when first Duarte and then Pedro married an Aragonese princess, the King of Castile began to worry. His land lay between Portugal and Aragon. Would there be a squeeze?

To avoid this, he tried to enlist Castile and Portugal in a common cause. "I am planning to invade Granada," he wrote Duarte, "and to drive the last Moslems from the peninsula. Will you and the Portuguese join me?"

Duarte had to make a decision, and the decision was a difficult one, for the advice he received was conflicting.

"March with him!" cried his nephew, the Count of Ourem. "At the least, you will gain the good will of this neighbor, and at best, you might be able to keep Granada or be given the Canaries."

But the Bishop of Oporto urged caution. "Stay at home," he told Duarte, "and attend to home matters. Particularly, deal with the unrest which has arisen among the nobility." They, the wise bishop knew, were already seething because of the taxes that they knew Duarte would soon be obliged to impose. Perhaps worse, the common people seethed too. "Do not pick someone else's chestnuts out of the fire."

Duarte compromised. He did nothing. He simply did not answer the King of Castile's letter. If he changed his mind, he could answer later.

The third problem could not be shuffled off so easily, for

it was created by the dreams and longings of a member of his own family, those of his youngest brother, Dom Fernando—and later, Henry, too.

Because of poor health and because he was much younger than his brothers, Dom Fernando took little part in the affairs of the kingdom while his father was alive. Instead, he lived the quiet life of a country gentleman on his two modest estates near Santarém, reading *The Lives of the Saints* and the *Sermons of St. Augustine* and on his birthday clothing as many of the poor as he was years old.

But when Duarte became king all this ended, for hardly had the latter put on the crown when he summoned Fernando into his presence.

"You are thirty-one," he told his brother. "I now make you the Master of the Knights of Avis." (This was the office João held before he became King of Portugal.)

Dom Fernando bowed his head and thanked Duarte, but almost immediately he was filled with discontent.

He said so, and he said so emphatically, for it did not seem right for him to be given this honor without earning it.

"I, master of this renowned military order, and my own knighthood purely honorary! But you, brother and Sire, and Pedro and Henry, too, won your knighthoods on the field of battle. It is not seemly."

"What would you do then?" asked Duarte.

"Go abroad," replied Fernando. "To England. To the Low Countries. To France. To Germany. To Hungary. To Constantinople, even. Go abroad and win glory. If you ever need me, I will come back again. I will come back, even if they make me Emperor of Greece or Emperor of Germany."

"Do not ask me that," replied Duarte, "for if you leave Portugal so soon after I have been crowned, people will say that we have quarreled."

"Then let me go to Africa with a Portuguese fleet and army. Let me go to Ceuta, and from Ceuta conquer Tangier. If I conquer Tangier, people can only say that I am serving you."

Again Duarte was in doubt and summoned advisers—his older half brother, the Count of Barcelos; Dom Pedro; Dom Henrique—Prince Henry, that is; and Dom João. With one exception, they opposed the idea. Their arguments were all the same: honor commands one thing, common sense another. Let common sense guide us.

Henry was the one exception. He had recently taken a new motto—IDA in place of *talent de bien faire*. He said that IDA stood for Infante Dom Anrique (Henrique or Henry), but *ida* is also the Portuguese word for expedition.

"You say that our kingdom is too small and poor for such a venture!" he cried. "Then let us make it larger and richer.

"If you still have any doubts," he continued, "consult your queen."

Henry felt safe in saying this, for he knew that anything Pedro opposed, she would favor. His wife's father had fought Leonora's father for the Castilian throne.

Henry was right.

"What!" was her reply to her husband when he went to her. "You do not wish to be King of Morocco and of Fez as well as King of Portugal?"

Duarte gave in.

"But I cannot give you the great army and the mighty fleet you ask for," he told Henry. Because of his experience, Henry rather than Fernando had been placed in command of the venture. But, of course, Fernando would go with him. "I cannot give you what we had when we took Ceuta. You know the array we had then. But now I can give you only fourteen thousand men, and of these only four thousand will be mounted."

"I will make do with them," was Henry's answer.

Duarte then ordered the preparations to begin.

Begin they did, late in 1436—this time in the open, for now secrecy was not essential as it would be assumed that the men and ships were to reinforce the Portuguese already in Africa. And so zealously was the outfitting and mustering carried out that by midsummer of 1437 the new armada was ready. Sometime after July 13 it set sail, once again from Restello. It reached Ceuta on August 26.

However, not even half of the fourteen thousand men who had been promised Henry were on board. His host numbered only six thousand, and of these only a thousand were mounted. To begin with, the Portuguese did not have enough shipping to transport any more, and their efforts to charter vessels in England, Germany, and the Biscay ports of France had not been successful. The three countries needed their ships for their own wars. Nor did volunteers step forward with the same eagerness they had shown two decades earlier. Twenty years of peace—twenty years to work at their farms and their neglected fishing—had made the Portuguese less eager to leave their homeland than they had been in King João's days.

"It is not enough," cried Governor Menezes, who met them when they had anchored. "Wait until Duarte sends reinforcements."

But Henry would not wait. "My men may be few, but they are the best in the land and in Christendom," he replied. He named some of them: two grandsons of Nun'Álvares; the royal marshal, Vasco Fernandes Coutinho; Captain Alvaro Vaz de Almada, who had fought at Agincourt and been knighted there by Henry V; the governor's son, Duarte Menezes; Zarco, the discoverer of Madeira.

"Moreover, they and I are commanded by God. If I had even fewer men, I would pursue the end I came for!"

Rashly—for Henry could be rash as well as wise, and his own nephew had predicted that he could be counted on "to launch out on some weighty enterprise without being really prepared"—he disregarded Duarte's command not to travel inland and thus lose contact with the coast and his vessels. He could have moved his men from Ceuta to Tangier along the shore where the guns of his fleet would have protected him. Instead, he struck dramatically southward, overland, to take the undefended inland city of Tetuán. Only when this was done did he march across a wild, monkey-infested spur of the Atlas Mountains to his objective.

He reached Tangier on Friday, September 13—even then Friday the 13th was considered unlucky—and having been told by refugees that the Moors were abandoning the city, ordered a prompt attack. However, the Moors were not fleeing (it was probably a story the defenders themselves had spread) and the Portuguese were driven back with heavy losses. They returned to their camp in chagrin and reported another evil omen. In the assault, Henry's banner had been torn to shreds by a sudden gust of wind.

Then Henry made another mistake.

"Since we cannot take Tangier by storm," he cried, "we must besiege it. Move up closer to its walls and set up barricades and dig trenches."

At these orders, the army went forward, and once again they moved so far inland that the Moors were able to come between them and their vessels.

The outcome should surprise no one. The Portuguese fought valiantly, and once even broke down two of the city's gates. They could not force an entrance, however. They dragged up protecting mantelets and ladders, but the defenders burned them down with tar and lighted tow. Next, led by the valiant Bishop of Ceuta, who was in full armor and brandished a sword instead of a crosier, they pushed up a portable wooden tower in which they hoped to shelter their crossbowmen. They even mounted a huge cannon and for as long as their powder lasted—they had only six barrels of it—they pounded the city with great stone cannon balls.

But seventy thousand of the enemy, commanded by Henry's old adversary Salah ben Salah, now held the shore, and an antlike swarm of Berbers (one frightened Portuguese said they numbered half a million) poured down from the hills. The besiegers became the besieged. Henry was trapped.

At first, he tried to break through the surrounding ring of foes. But although his men held their ground from dawn to dusk, they could not shatter the ring that encircled them. Next, Henry laid plans for a break-through during the night, but one of his chaplains defected to the foe and told them what the Portuguese were going to do. Finally he had no choice but to master his pride and send an emissary to Salah to ask for the terms of an armistice. Cut off from their ships for many weeks, his men had neither provisions nor water. They had been reduced to eating the flesh of their horses (half raw because they had only the straw in their saddlebags to fuel the fires) and quenching their thirst by pressing wet mud to their lips.

Salah's terms were not harsh, despite the fact that his Berber tribesmen allies did not want him to offer any terms at all. They wanted to be allowed to slaughter the invaders down to the last Portuguese.

"Yield Ceuta to me and surrender all your Moorish prisoners. Make peace for one hundred years and swear this on the book that you call holy. And as security, give us one of the royal princes as hostage. I," he added generously, "will give you one of my sons."

What could Henry do but accept? He had to. And then came

the heart-wringing question: Which of the princes would serve as hostage?

"I will go," said Henry. "I should go, since it was my doing and not doing that brought us to this pass. And besides, it was I who pledged to yield Ceuta, and it is I who can find ways to break that pledge."

But his captains would not have it.

"You are our commander in chief. It would humble Portugal into the dust if we surrendered you. Besides that—we may yet need your skill in battle."

Since Dom Pedro and Dom João were both in Portugal, there remained only Dom Fernando.

Henry looked at his brother.

"It is my duty," said Fernando, clasping his pale hands in front of the cross which always hung before his breast. (There are some who say he always wished to be a martyr—that he desired this even more than he desired knighthood.)

Word was sent to Salah, and that very evening the Moor himself rode up leading the horse that was to carry off the royal hostage. The two brothers embraced with deep feeling and then Dom Fernando mounted and rode off beside his captor. It was dusk and he soon disappeared into the shadows. Of their own free will, seven of his loyal followers accompanied him. Except for them, no other Portuguese would ever again see the Constant Prince—Fernando was called this because he endured so steadfastly the cruelties and hardships to which he would be subjected.

That does not mean that Henry and Duarte did not do everything possible to secure his release. Everything except give up Ceuta, that is. First Henry told Salah that the truce had been broken. This was true. The Moor's own troops did obey his orders, but his camel-riding Berber allies refused to give up their right to massacre and plunder. Henry and his men had to fight their way to the ships, which had followed them to Tangier.

These took him to Ceuta and from there he sent a message to Salah.

"You have not kept the agreed-on terms, and so the treaty is no longer in effect. Send Fernando back to me. I will send back your son."

"I have sufficient sons, and can beget more if needed," replied Salah. "Fernando will be returned when I have Ceuta."

Next Henry sent Dom João down the Atlantic coast of Morocco with a fleet. He had been told that Fernando had been taken to Arzila, a small Moorish seaport, and João was to make a show of force before it, and if he could, attempt to recapture his brother. Unfortunately, however, the autumn gales had already begun to blow and they drove João's ships away from the shore.

After that, Henry himself went back to Portugal. (But not to Lisbon. Henry said he would not come to the court with Fernando still in Moorish hands, and met his brother near Évora.) Clad in deepest mourning, he there begged Duarte for a new army of twenty-four thousand men. With this, he could rescue Fernando. But Duarte knew that such an army could not be raised easily—or in time—and shrugged off the suggestion.

Finally, Henry persuaded Duarte to convene the *cortes* (his parliament), and have it meet with the royal princes and the noblemen of the land at Leiria. This Duarte did, and asked for permission to surrender the city that Salah ben Salah wanted so badly. The debate was vehement. Representatives from Lisbon and Oporto—both with trading fleets which used Ceuta as a port of call—said that the idea of giving it up was preposterous, but those from the smaller fishing ports and the inland farming cities said: "Hand it over!"

The princes and the noblemen were not of one mind either.

"Give it up," said Dom Pedro, "and abandon all foolish efforts to set up a North African empire." In his opinion, Fernando was worth more than a city which some said cost Portugal nearly thirty thousand ducats a year to maintain.

"No," argued the Count of Arriolos, "to yield Ceuta would be a shame and disgrace, nor would Dom Fernando wish us to do this."

But the clinching argument came from the primate of all Spain, the Archbishop of Braga.

"Ceuta is a Christian city," he said, "and has been for more than twenty years. It would be a heinous crime to surrender a Christian city to the infidel without the Pope's permission." But it was obvious that the Pope (Eugenius IV), who was trying to show the Eastern Church that the Roman Church was great and powerful, would never grant this.

Although he hoped with all his heart and soul to win his brother's release, Duarte did not dare oppose the wishes of these two churchmen. Once again he did nothing and Dom Fernando continued to languish in his prison.

Duarte had been even more shaken by the Tangier disaster than Henry had. He, too, blamed himself for it; he was king and could have forbidden the expedition. He was at Carnide not far from Lisbon when the tidings of the disaster of Tangier were brought to him by Alvaro Vaz, who decked himself out in his gayest clothes and cried that chimes should be rung out in honor of the valiant deeds done at Tangier rather than somber bells of mourning for those lost there. For a moment, Duarte seemed heartened but gloom swiftly enveloped him and he wandered like a lost soul from Lisbon to Leiria to Évora and then to Tomár.

There late in August 1438 he fell ill in the ancient castle and on September 9 he died. At that time, plague raged in the land

and it was said that he was one of its victims. His doctors thought otherwise. Duarte's death, they said, "was caused by two days' fever which resulted from his unequaled sorrow and distress at his misfortunes." In other words, he died of a broken heart.

Henry was at his side. Forgetting his vow not to appear at the court until Dom Fernando had been set free, he galloped north at breakneck speed and reached Duarte's bedside. He reached it only in time to bid his brother farewell.

After Duarte had died, Henry remained in the north only long enough to perform one final service for this king and elder brother, whose death he often felt he had caused.

The new King of Portugal was Duarte's son, Affonso V, then six years old, and in his will, Duarte had made Queen Leonora regent. But the Portuguese would not be ruled by a woman, least of all by a Spanish woman, and they threatened a revolt.

Henry offered this solution. Leonora would be guardian of her children, and Dom Pedro, now the oldest living brother, would be named Defender of the Realm. In other words, there would be two regents—one for family affairs and the other for state affairs.

It was a compromise, and like most compromises, did not completely please anybody. But it was the best that could be done under the circumstances, and it worked—or at least it worked for a while. Dom Pedro accepted it cheerfully and the queen said she did.

Then Henry, having shown that he was a statesman even if he was no general, returned to Sagres, and this time he meant to stay. For he now realized that his life mission was and should be to make his captains press on ever farther and farther, and not to fight wars in Africa, or even help run Portugal.

It was also, he thought, the best way to help pay his debt to Dom Fernando.

In his chronicle, *The Discovery and Conquest of Guinea*, Azurara gives "five reasons why the Lord Infante was moved to command" these voyages. Here are two of them.

"During the long years Henry had fought against the Moors, he had never found a Christian king nor a lord outside of Portugal who would aid him in the said wars." If he did find one, says Azurara, such a king might become an important ally. And obviously, Henry must have reasoned, such an ally might help free Fernando.

"His great desire was to make increase in the faith of our Lord Jesus Christ and to bring to Him all the souls that could possibly be saved." If he could not free Fernando, at least then he would have served the faith for which his brother had suffered. It is true that Henry was moved most of all by his burning love of discovery. But if at the same time he could advance the cause which meant so much to the Constant Prince, that would be an added glory. And it might ease his conscience too.

In the meantime, Dom Fernando's treatment grew steadily worse. He and his companions were indeed taken to Arzila. They were driven there like cattle, in fact, and when they arrived, "faint with hunger and half blind with thirst," a crowd surged out to stone them and spit at them. Then they were handed over to the cruel vizier of the King of Fez. For three months, they were shut up in the mouldering, unlighted rooms of an old broken-down castle, except when, bound by chains, they were taken out and set to work in the royal stables and royal gardens. For clothes they had nothing but rags. Fernando himself was left with only a shirt. Even his doublet with two hundred ducats sewed into its lining had been stolen from him. For food they had bread, but no wine. For bedding they had bundles of filthy straw which they had raked from the horses' stalls.

Finally, when letters directed to Fernando and hinting at a

possible rescue were intercepted, Fernando was deprived of even the consolation of seeing the sunlight as he toiled. He was now separated from his companions and shut up in a cell so small that he could not stand in it. Indeed he could scarcely even lie down. It swarmed with vermin too, and although he was allowed a lamp by which to read his breviary, he could only glimpse his friends and the outside world through a small hole in the wall where he had pried out a loose brick. A living skeleton, his skin like dry parchment, his body cramped and deformed, he lived in this wretched manner for the last fifteen months of his life.

Nor, when at last he died on July 5, 1443, were his mortal remains treated any better. The Portuguese had at last offered a huge ransom, and the vizier had just refused it in the hope of getting an even larger one, when Fernando died. By dying, "the infidel dog" had cheated the vizier, and he fell into a fury. He ordered the poor wasted body be dragged from its cell and hanged head downward from the city wall. This was done, but somehow during the night one of Dom Fernando's servitors managed to steal his master's heart. Eight years later, it was smuggled to Portugal where it was buried beside Fernando's father and mother at Batalha. Pilgrims often knelt before the tomb it lay in, for Fernando was soon regarded as a saint.

Henry's Caravels

Not long before Dom Fernando's death Henry began sending out his ships once again. Except for the first of them, however, they were no longer the kind used by Gil Eannes and Affonso Gonçalves Baldaya. The prince navigator always insisted on the best—the best and most modern navigating instruments, the best and most recently revised maps and charts, the most detailed and accurate sailing directions. He insisted on the best ships, too.

As his explorers went farther and farther down the coast of Africa, he turned to his ship designers and shipbuilders. "Come up with something more useful and more manageable than the barca or the barinel," he instructed them. The result was the caravel.

Since the days when man floated down the Nile or the Euphrates in a reed boat, he has developed many types of vessels and some are still renowned: the Greek or Roman trireme, the Viking long ship, the Venetian galley, the Spanish galleon, the English and Dutch East-Indiamen, the Yankee clipper, and finally the modern ocean greyhound. (The first of these was the *Mauretania*, which from 1907 to 1929 held all transatlantic speed records; the most recent is the *United States*, which crossed from Sandy Hook, New York, to England in less than four days.)

None of these, however, played a more important role in the history of seafaring than the new type of vessel which first put in an appearance around 1440 in Portugal, and almost certainly at the urging of Henry.

The caravel was everything a seafarer could ask for. Probably developed from an ancestor of the oil barges and wine barges that still ply the Douro and the Tagus, it was roomy, and compared to the other vessels of the day, comfortable. For example, even the first caravels (they were called *caravelas latinas* to distinguish them from the later, larger *caravelas redondas* such as Columbus's *Niña*) were rarely less than fifty tons burden. They were usually over one hundred feet long and had a beam of from thirty to forty feet.

Despite this, they could be sailed by a relatively small crew. This was because they were three-masted and each of their lateen sails could be trimmed separately. The lateen sail, invented by the Arabs, was a triangular one carried on a long, slanting yard. By contrast, the barca and the barinel were basically singlestickers and the one square sail they normally carried had to be larger than those of the caravel. It thus required more manpower to handle.

The caravel was also swift, and because its pine planks (supported by oaken frames) were fitted edge to edge—we still call a ship constructed in this way carvel-built—instead of overlapping (lapstreak or clinker-built), it slipped through the water with little disturbance. The rudder hung from a square stern, which made it easy to maneuver.

"Caravels," said a Venetian who knew them, "are the

finest ships that sail the sea, and there is nowhere they cannot go."

There were two reasons for this. The caravel could sail closer-hauled—i.e., point closer toward the direction from which the wind came—than any other type of vessel built so far. (It is probable that neither the barca nor the barinel could sail to windward at all.) The caravel also had a flatter bottom and its shoal draft made it less likely to ground upon an uncharted shoal or sandbank; because of this, it dared to push fearlessly into tangled mangrove swamps through which only narrow, twisting channels run.

Nevertheless—and in spite of the fact that caravels were now being built—the vessel that Henry sent out when he resumed his explorations was either a barca or a barinel. In the spring of 1441, "the affairs of the realm being somewhat more settled though not fully quieted," he ordered a "little ship" to be fitted out and gave it to one Antão Gonçalves, "his chamberlain and a very young man." Antão's official orders were to sail to Africa and there "to ship a cargo of sea-lion skins and sea-lion oil." Unofficially it must have been hinted that it would be greatly appreciated if he did what Baldaya had not been able to do—bring back a native captive or so.

A caravel, however, followed swiftly on Antão's heels. Henry had decided that hints were not enough, and that anyway, even if he understood them, Antão was hardly the man to carry them out. And so hardly had he disappeared over the horizon when Henry ordered one of the new vessels to be equipped. He gave its command to another of his young knights, Nuno Tristão, who like Antão "had been brought up from early boyhood in Henry's own chambers," but unlike him, had already won his spurs in battle and was noted for his courage and zeal.

To Nuno nothing was said of either sea-lion skins or oil.

"Go," he was commanded, "as far as you can beyond Punta Galha"—the last place the Portuguese had reached before Henry called off all voyages in 1437—"and there bestir yourself to capture some of the people of the country so that I may learn about it."

Nuno obeyed gladly. Out into the ocean he sailed. Past Cape Noun. Past Cape Juby. Even past Cape Bojador. Finally he sighted Cape Deception, sailed southwestward for some twenty-one miles, and rounded present-day Point Durnford into the Río de Oro. There, all these miles from home and at anchor before a drying sandbank, lay a small but sturdy vessel flying Henry's banner. It was Antão's "little ship" and near its stern stood Antão himself, wildly waving and capering with joy.

"I have done all that my lord commanded me to," he replied. "All and more! In my hold are the sea-lion skins and oil I was bidden to ship here, but I also—see them beside me—have two people of the land. Finally, that which he wished for so long! Now tell me of Portugal and of Henry and of my friends and relatives."

He was almost ecstatic with pride.

Nuno was not. He looked across the water from his vessel to the other vessel. Yes, there were prisoners, all right. Antão had done what Baldaya had not done, and what Henry wanted. But what prisoners! A decrepit camel herder clad in rags—and he had been taken only because he was wounded as he tried to flee—and a wretched old woman, who, it turned out, was really a Negro slave. (The natives of the place, as the Portuguese would soon find out, were not Negroes, but Assenegs, related to the Tuaregs, a Berber people.) It was farcical, but how could he say this without hurting Antão's feelings?

"It is good," Nuno told Antão, "but it is not good enough. And I have done nothing. Of surety, I say to you that I would hold myself disgraced if I and my men did not help you gain greater booty than this to bring back to Prince Henry. Let us land then and take it."

Antão raised an objection. "But the people of the land now know we are here. We cannot surprise them."

"What of it?" cried Nuno. "Are we not soldiers of Christ? Are we not Portuguese?"

His lieutenants supported him, and so did Antão's lieutenants.

Thus encouraged, Nuno waited until dark. Then he and Antão and an armed party got into one of the ship's boats and were rowed ashore with muffled oars. They marched southward until they came upon two encampments not very far apart. These they attacked simultaneously, shouting "Portugal!" and "São Tiago!" at the top of their voices. The surprise was complete and the inhabitants scattered, only a few making even a show of defending themselves. Nuno killed one of them, and in this first battle between Europeans and people living south of the Atlas Mountains, his men slew three.

They also rounded up ten prisoners, men, women, and boys. One prisoner was an important one. He was an Asseneg chieftain named Adahu, who, says Azurara, "had been to other lands, where he had learned the Moorish tongue." On Nuno's ship, there was an Arab who could understand him.

With their prisoners the party returned to the two ships, and then and there, over Antão's protests, Nuno knighted Antão, saying that he had fought well even if he had opposed the expedition. He named the place where they had actually landed the Porto do Cavaleiro. This done, he directed Antão to return to Portugal with the men and women they had taken. "I must continue," Nuno said. "I have been ordered to." Then as his fellow captain was lost to sight, Nuno careened his ship as calmly as if he had been in Lisbon harbor, had his men scrape the barnacles off her bottom, and floated her at the next high tide. After that, he worked his way southward until he saw ahead of him a long, low, gleaming promontory. He anchored under its cliffs and named it Cabo Branco (White Cape), now Cape Blanc.

Then—and only because he had run out of provisions—he turned north. But he was now more than a thousand miles distant from Cape St. Vincent and had gone a good hundred miles farther than any other of Henry's captains. His journey home was uneventful. But when he reached Portugal, he found the land agog.

It was agog because Henry had received Adahu with the honors the desert chieftain believed to be his due, and Adahu had begun to talk. He told Henry of the mysterious desert which stretched endlessly from the Atlantic Ocean to the Red Sea and from Tunis and Algeria to the tropical jungles. It was so wide, he said, that no one man had ever crossed it. Then he told of the caravans that plied its rocks and sands. Sometimes they consisted of as many as three hundred camels. But even these ships of the desert could not endure the blazing heats and midnight freezing colds. Even they had to travel in relays. One caravan would go just so far and then be replaced by another caravan. But they all carried the world's most precious cargo—the bright, yellow metal men have fought for ever since they knew of it.

"Where do they get this gold?" asked Henry.

"No one knows," replied the Asseneg. "It is bartered for salt, where the desert meets the jungle. The salt is piled in heaps at an agreed-on spot. When the pile is big enough, it disappears and gold is left in its place."

"But who are the barterers?"

"No one knows," said Adahu again, "but we think they are the Negroes—the black men who live in the jungle."

"They are Moslem as are you Assenegs?"

"No, they are idol-worshipping, witch-worshipping heathens. They are fit only to be slaves. When we can, we enslave them."

Then Adahu, seeing that he had an audience, launched a farrago of fact mixed with fable that made Henry's courtiers stare. There were huge inland oceans in the heart of Africa, he said. (Maybe he was thinking of lakes such as Tanganyika and Victoria, which would have seemed like oceans to a desert nomad.) There was also a great Negro empire called Melli, or Mali. (There had been. Ruled by the king of the Mandingo people, it flourished from 1235 to 1433, when Moslem Tuaregs from the Sahara captured its capital, Timbuktu, and set up their own empire. Timbuktu was the center of the gold and kola nut trade. Some say that at one time its population was 1,000,000.) There was a western Nile that rose in the Mountains of the Moon near the source of the eastern Nile. (This was not true. The western Nile was the Niger. It rose near the Atlantic Ocean, flowed east for a while, and then turned south to discharge its waters into the Gulf of Guinea. But the fable of the western Nile had been believed since the days of the Greek and Roman geographers.) Finally, somewhere in the interior of the continent lived a race of dog-headed men. These probably were baboons.

Henry listened attentively, his chin cupped in his hands. Even after tales which were impossible or even improbable had been discounted, here was proof of everything he had dreamed about since Ceuta—that there were cities rich in gold, and that Africa was a wealthy continent.

Forthwith he wrote Pope Eugenius IV—a Venetian, Gabriele Condulmero, who needed all the help he could get in his struggle to maintain papal supremacy.

"Between where my ships have sailed, Your Holiness, and

the realm of Prester John, there is a vast and wealthy land inhabited by heathens. Will you give jurisdiction of it to the Order of Christ? And will you also bestow the same indulgences that you bestow on crusaders to those sailing there or fighting there?"

"Eugenius the Bishop [of Rome]," came the answer, did now "concede and grant" all that Henry had asked for; it added, "Let no one break or contradict this order or mandate." The penalty: he who did so would "lie under the curse of the Almighty God and of the blessed Apostles St. Peter and St. Paul."

Henry received more practical help from closer at hand. Acting as regent, his brother Dom Pedro gave him a charter by which he granted him "the whole of the fifth of the profits which appertained to the king" and further provided that no one could sail to the "new found lands" without Henry's permission.

Now Henry and his captains could reap their rewards on earth as well as in heaven. As a result, vessel after vessel went out.

In 1443, Antão Gonçalves, still in his "little ship," sailed for the Río de Oro again. With him was a German knight, Balthasar. Balthasar, who had fought with Henry at Ceuta, wanted to take part in the discoveries everybody was talking about, and he also wanted to witness a storm at sea. "I can tell about it when I return to the court of my master, the Emperor Frederick III," he said.

This wish was granted. Hardly had Antão left Sagres when he encountered winds so violent and waves so huge, he reported to Henry, "that it was a marvel they escaped destruction."

On board too, in a tent pitched just abaft the mainmast, was the tall-talking Adahu and two of the other captives.

Adahu had promised that if they put him ashore near where he had been captured, not only would his followers pay a great ransom, but he would convince them that they should trade with the Portuguese.

He was indeed put ashore and that was the last that was ever heard of him. It was a different matter with the other two. They remained aboard Antão's ship, and a week later a band of one hundred rode up and offered ten black slaves in exchange for them. The offer was accepted, and the men on the shore thereupon threw in a bag of gold dust, an oxhide shield, and a number of ostrich eggs as a bonus.

Even the ostrich eggs were carried back to Henry. Three omelets were made of them, and these, it was said, were "as fresh and as good as if they had been the eggs of a domestic fowl." That is hard to believe.

In the same year, Nuno Tristão made his second voyage. Once again he commanded a caravel. Indeed, from now on only caravels were used. He reached Cape Blanc and went on for another twenty-five leagues until he came to a low, sandy island which he called Gete. (Today, it is known as Arguin.) Here, he and his men saw a new sight. Twenty-five canoes came into sight, aboard them a number of natives who straddled the hulls and used their feet for paddles.

Beyond Gete they came to another island, "on which were an infinity of royal herons." Since these were easily caught, Nuno's men "found great refreshment" there, and from then on almost every Portuguese ship touched at *Ilha des Garças*, (Heron Island), as they named it.

In 1445, Henry's first fleet went out. It consisted of six armed caravels and was commanded by one Lançarote, who was the royal tax-collector in Lagos and who, as "a man of great good sense, understood the profit he would be able to gain." But although he hoped to make money, he explored too, and went on to the Island of Tiger (now Tidra), which was about thirty miles south of Heron Island.

In 1445, too, Nuno Tristão went to Arguin, and then to Tidra, and finding that both islands were now deserted, continued in the hope that he would come to the *Terra dos Negros* (Land of Blacks), where the great tropical forest began.

He almost did. "Up to then," he reported—that is, up to the time he had rounded Cape Timiris just before Tidra—"the land had been sandy and untilled and treeless, but this new land was covered with palms and other green and beautiful trees." It is clear that he was approaching the mouth of the Sénégal, which is still thought of as dividing the desert from the jungle.

Later in the same year Diniz Dias went even farther. Without ever "lowering sail"—without touching at any port, that is—he sailed straight for "the land of Guinea" (a term used in those days to describe any part of West Africa south of the Sénégal). As he neared it, said Diniz, "some of the people of the land came out to meet us in a small boat made out of a hollow tree trunk like the *couchos* which our laborers use to cross the rapids of the Mondego and the Zêzere rivers in wintertime." They wanted to see whether the apparition which floated so loftily on the sea was a fish, or a phantom, or a great bird. They paid for their curiosity. Four of them were taken prisoner.

After that Diniz continued until he came to a long, relatively high promontory which thrusts farther to the west than any other point in Africa, and since the scrubby underbrush with which two of its hills were covered seemed green after the desert coast farther north, he named it Cape Verde.

In 1446, Nuno Tristão made a third voyage. He reached Cape Verde and went on for another fifty leagues. But he was slain—as were most of his men—by the poisoned arrows of a band of natives at the mouth of "a great river," which was almost certainly the Gambia.

Finally, in 1448, Alvaro Ferndandes sailed past both Cape Verde and the Cape of Masts (Alvaro had named it this on an earlier voyage because of two storm-stripped palm trees he had found there) and continued until he had gone another one hundred miles farther than Nuno had. This took him at least as far as what is now Portuguese Guinea, and probably farther. He was rewarded generously for this distance record. Dom Pedro gave him one hundred *dobras* and Henry gave him a second hundred. This made him a rich man.

These, of course, were not the only expeditions which Henry sent out. The voyages described here are those which went just a little farther than any voyage made before them. But Azurara says that by 1446, fifty-one caravels had sailed to Africa, and for once his figure is probably low. They had reached a point four hundred leagues beyond Cape Bojador. That is farther beyond the once impassable cape than Bojador is distant from Sagres. In the next two years, at least fifteen more caravels went out. They sailed at least one hundred and fifty miles farther.

The men who commanded them were of all sorts—grooms of the palace, well-born noble youths from Henry's household, important merchants; also, the master of the royal galley, the treasurer of Ceuta, one of the assayers of the royal mint, and a seafaring bishop whose ship unfortunately ran aground. There was even a noble Dane, one Vallarte (Vollert or Abelhart), a gentleman from the court of King Christopher III of Norway, Denmark, and Sweden.

The tales they brought back were as varied as the men themselves, some of them as fascinating and as hard to believe as the tales told by Adahu. They spoke of the unfamiliar animals they had seen: the elephant, twice as tall as a man, with long tusks worth more than gold and a tough and useful hide; the wild buffalo; the antelope; the great apes.

They described strange birds. The ostrich with its white tail- and wing-plumes had, they said, long bare legs which enabled it to outrun a horse. The flamingo, with its short feathers (nothing was said of its pink color) and small head, had a beak so large that "its neck was not able to support the weight of it." The hornbill's beak was a cubit or more long—a cubit is eighteen inches. The beaks, it was reported, "look like the engraved sheaths of swords and the maw is so big that the leg of a man could go into it up to the knee."

New fish were also described—the remora, for one, with "a crown on its head." This is really a suction disk by which the fish can attach itself to a shark or to anything else that moves.

Incredible trees were reported too. The baobab, never more than seventy feet tall, had a trunk often thirty feet in circumference. "It had to be seen to be believed," said one of Henry's captains, and he told of one, by no means the largest, which measured "one hundred palms around the trunk. It bore a gourdlike fruit with seeds as big as hazelnuts." Henry's captains spoke also of the stately silk-cotton trees, from whose fibers the natives wove a crude cloth.

Not even the heavens were the same, said the commander of one vessel. The stars were so bright that you could recognize a man's face by starlight. Other captains reported that the constellations which they knew and the North Star sank ever lower and lower toward the horizon and were replaced by new constellations. What could they use for guides now?

The men who saw all these sights also had adventure after adventure. Not all had happy endings.

Vallarte the Dane, for example, refused to take the advice of his Portuguese interpreter, and allowed himself to be lured ashore near Cape Verde in the hope of seeing a live elephant. He had already seen "an elephant's teeth [tusks]," but that was not enough.

At a native banquet consisting of a she-goat, a kid, couscous (a dish of meat and semolina), native bread, native corn, and palm wine, he asked Guitanye, the local chief, if he would find an elephant for him.

"If you do," Vallarte promised, "I will give you a tent made of linen cloth large enough to shelter twenty-five to thirty, yet so light that one man can carry it on his back."

Off went Guitanye, and for two days neither he nor any other native was seen. Then a single black man, carrying a gourd filled with wine or water, came to the water's edge. He seemed to be signaling.

"My elephant, or at least news of it!" cried Vallarte and ordered the crew of the ship's boat to row him to the shore. This they did—and then catastrophe! The man waiting for him dropped the gourd—this was a signal—and with that the beach swarmed with howling tribesmen shaking their weapons.

Only then did Vallarte realize his danger. "Row!" he shouted, and the men plied their oars, but a wave threw the boat back onto the beach and they were all prisoners.

All but one. He jumped into the sea and swam desperately toward the caravel.

"I looked back three or four times," he said, "and as I did, I could see that only one man had been slain and that Vallarte was still sitting in the stern of the boat."

That was the last time the Dane was ever seen. But many years later, "some captives who were natives of that part" were brought to Henry and they told him that "in a castle far inland were Christians, of whom three were still living." Was one of them Vallarte?

Gonçalo de Sintra also came to a bad end, and he too brought it on himself. He was one of Henry's young men, stout-hearted and sturdy, and his orders were explicit. "Go straight to Guinea and for nothing fail of this." But hoping for "advantages" as well as honor, and against the advice of the others on his ship, he went instead to Naar, one of the islands in Arguin Bay. There, he thought, it would be easy to capture a human cargo. On arrival, he beached his vessel, scrambled ashore with a party of twelve men, and in the dark of the moon marched along the beach toward a native village he had been told of.

Presently, the party came to a small creek, which, because it was low tide, they crossed easily. But when, having found neither village nor inhabitants, they attempted to return, they discovered that the tide had flooded and they could no longer ford the river. Weighed down with their armor, they could not swim across either. What could they do then but sit patiently on the bank and wait for low tide? This they did, but the tide ebbed slowly, and the water was still deep when, just at dawn, they were attacked suddenly by a band of two hundred. Fighting "not in truth like a man who had forgotten his courage, but inflicting great injuries upon his enemies," Gonçalo was slain, as were seven of his followers. The other five managed to get across the creek and return to their caravel. Being now too shorthanded, "they had no inducement to go farther," and shortly made "sail for the kingdom."

Gonçalo and his men were the first Portuguese to lose their lives in West Africa. They would not be the last. And there were many others who had narrow escapes. One such was Martin Pereira, another "page of the Infante's household" who went to Africa. Near Cape Verde he found himself "in a very fierce combat" with "about forty Moors. . . . He toiled hard and his shield was like the back of a porcupine when it lifts its quills." But Martin was not even wounded. Another was Alvaro Fernandes. Alvaro was wounded by a poisoned arrow. But he smeared the wound with olive oil and theriac (a medieval cure-all) and stayed alive.

Not every adventure turned out badly, however, and two of them showed the stuff that Henry's men were made of.

João Fernandes's was the first. João, too, was one of Henry's youthful squires, and in 1444, "of his own free will," he decided to remain in Africa, "if only to see the country and bring back news of it to his prince." He was landed on the shores of the Río de Oro and his ship returned to Portugal. Seven months later the crew of a caravel, sent back in the hopes of finding him, saw a man frantically waving to them from the beach at a point fifty or sixty miles south of where João had been left behind. So blackened was he by the sun that they thought it was an Asseneg come to barter with them. But it was João. He had lived with the desert nomads all that time.

He had a story to tell, and he told it at once: "As soon as the ship which brought me from Portugal sailed away the Assenegs stripped me of everything I had—not only the biscuits and wheat that you left with me, but even my garments. But they did not leave me naked. They clad me in a burnoose [the white hooded robe worn by the Arabs]. It was better suited to the country, they said."

Thereafter—"for the Assenegs," said João, "never stay in one place more than a week"—they took him on a wild journey over miles and miles of desert where nothing grew but wicked-looking thorns and a few starved palm trees.

"We were mounted on camels, and on and on we went through the most barren country ever seen. In it there was nothing but sand and heat-split rocks, except on the banks of its few rivers or where there was an oasis. There there was some sparse grass and they would pause to let their livestock graze. Then they were on their way again, guided only by the wind and by the flights of birds or by the stars as sailors are."

"What were your hosts like?" João was asked by his rescuers.

"They are very poor and except along the coast where they eat fish, they live almost entirely on milk. Sometimes even that fails them. Once we were three days without even water. I thought that we would perish. But this did not keep them from pressing ever on, although the heat is so great that horses cannot endure it. They went either on foot or on camel back. They have plenty of camels—many of them white— and these camels can travel fifty leagues in a day."

"Why did they press on so?"

"They said that they were seeking a noble called Ahude Meymam who wished to traffic with them. He had black slaves to offer them. These Ahude had taken by thievery rather than by force"—in other words, he had kidnaped them —"for the Assenegs are not as good fighters as the Negroes are. They also could obtain gold from Ahude—this as well as hides, wool, butter, cheese, dates, amber, civet, and oil— for he was eager to trade with us."

"Where did this gold come from?"

João could only echo Adahu, the Asseneg chieftain brought to Henry by Antão Gonçalves. "From the Negro lands. They say there is a great kingdom there called Melli. But I do not know whether to believe this or not."

You may be sure that when João returned to Sagres and repeated his story, Henry listened to him as he had to the Asseneg chief. For here was a man who had traveled through thousands of miles of African wilderness and had heard tales of fantastic riches just beyond it. Once again what Henry had been told at Ceuta was confirmed.

Two years later another of Henry's followers performed a feat that was even more remarkable than João's. His name was

Ayres Tinocco, and since he is described as "a boy of Henry's household" he may have been as young as fourteen or fifteen years old.

When in 1446 Nuno Tristão and his men were attacked by Negroes armed with poisoned arrows, four were already dead by the time his band had returned to their caravel, and the rest—including Nuno—died very shortly afterward, and in great pain. Left alive were only the five who had remained aboard the ship: a sailor who could handle lines but knew nothing about navigation, two boys as young as Ayres, a young black captive, and Ayres. The five of them together did not have the strength even to raise the anchor, so they cut the cables; fortunately, the tide was ebbing, and they drifted out to sea.

Then Ayres took over. He was from the inland town of Olivenza, had been signed on as one of the ship's clerks, and knew no more of navigation than the sailor did. But he was an alert young man and a good listener, and he now remembered some of the things he had heard from Nuno and his officers.

"Let us put them into effect," he said. "Let us steer due north guided by the North Star, but ever and anon let us incline a little to the east of north. That way lies Portugal."

It did, but it was a good two thousand miles distant. Moreover, the winds were variable, and the handful of men still left could not always keep the sails trimmed to best advantage. And so they progressed slowly. One month went by. Six weeks. Then two months. To keep alive, they fished when they lay becalmed and caught water in a spare sail when there was a squall.

Then one day, just as they had about given up hope, they saw a long dark smudge on the horizon.

"Land! It must be land!" they cried.

But at the same time they saw also the sails of an approaching vessel. Its deck was crowded with a band of swarthy villains, all armed with scimitars.

"A pirate! It must be a pirate!" That was their next cry. It must be a Moorish xebec come out of Safi or some other Moroccan port. They would be taken to Tangier or Fez and sold as slaves.

It turned out to be a pirate indeed, but not a Moorish one. Suddenly, over the water came a hail and it was in Galician, the language of northwestern Spain, so like Portuguese that Ayres and his men could understand it.

"Ship ahoy! Who are you? Where do you come from?"

"From the land of Guinea. From beyond Cape Verde. We are seeking Sagres and Prince Henry. Where are we?"

"You are off Sines in southwest Portugal," cried Pero Falcão, the strange vessel's captain. "Follow me, and I will guide you to your master."

A day later Ayres's caravel lay at anchor under the Vila do Infante, and he himself went up the rugged footpath to tell the Infante of "the tragical outcome of their voyage" and also "of the multitude of arrows" by which Nuno and his men were slain.

He was alive to do this only because he had accomplished one of the most remarkable feats in the history of seafaring. An inexperienced and landlubber youth had brought a three-masted vessel at least ninety feet long from beyond the Sénégal to Portugal, and had done this without ever sighting land and with only four equally inexperienced helpers. It was an accomplishment hard to equal. Small wonder that the age that produced Ayres—while it was also producing great captain after great captain—became known as the Golden Age of Prince Henry the Navigator. It was certainly navigation's golden age.

Yet this golden age had at least one serious blot upon its

scutcheon. It saw the beginning of European slave trade in Africa. To be sure, at first this trade was only a trickle. Between 1441 and 1448, for example, only 927 men, women, and children were brought to Portugal, whereas when the English and the Dutch—and the Americans—took over slave trading, they sometimes carried as many as seventy thousand human beings to Latin America alone in a single year. It is true, too, that Henry never encouraged this practice and that he only tolerated it because it was a way of converting heathens into Christians, and thus, according to the belief of the day, saving their souls from hell.

But the fact is that this business of dealing with our fellow men as if they were so much merchandise or so many cattle began—at least as far as Europe is concerned—with Henry's captains.

The first slave auction in Europe was held in Portugal, too. It took place in Lagos on August 8, 1445. Azurara describes it.

"The two hundred and thirty captives were taken ashore in boats, and hot as the day was, they were marched into an open field. It was a sight to see. Some of them were white as we are, others were less white like mulattoes; others again were black as Ethiops.

"What heart could be so hard as not to be pierced with piteous feeling? For some kept their heads low and their faces bathed in tears. Some groaned very dolorously and looked up to heaven. Some struck their faces with their palms and then flung themselves at full length upon the ground. Others lamented as in a dirge, after the custom of their country. And then came what was truly lamentable. A drawing was made, and it was necessary to separate fathers from sons, husbands from wives, brothers from brothers."

At this, pandemonium broke out.

"Sons rushed to their fathers, and mothers to their babes.

They flung themselves to the ground, willing to accept blows if only their flesh was not torn from them."

Azurara himself was shaken and moved.

"O thou God," he cried, "I pray that my tears may not wrong my conscience [namely, his knowledge that they would be made Christians]! For if brute beasts understand the sufferings of their kind, what wouldst Thou have me do? Are not these poor souls the sons of Adam even as we?"

In all fairness, it should be pointed out that most people in the land shared his feelings, and in general, the slaves were well treated in Portugal. They were well clothed, well fed, and always taught some trade, and since the thought that black was different from white hardly existed in fourteenth-century Portugal, slaves often intermarried "with the people of the land." Moreover, unlike Moslem captives, the black Africans rarely tried to flee, but rather "in time forgot their own country." Most of their sons and daughters and all their grandchildren thought of themselves as Portuguese.

Slavery, moreover, was widely practiced, and although the inhumanity associated with it was frequently deplored, it was widely accepted in those days. It was, for example, the normal fate of a prisoner of war, as the story of Dom Fernando makes plain. But over and above that, the buying and selling of human beings, despite often-expressed and strenuous papal objections, was engaged in by almost every maritime nation. And one does not get very far in studying and understanding history if one tries to judge another period and other peoples by the standards of today.

Nevertheless, the carrying on of this sordid business by Henry's captains can only be considered a blot—all the more since some of its tragic consequences are still plaguing us five centuries later.

The Voyages of the Venetian, Cadamosto

After the capture of Vallarte the Dane in 1447, Henry did not send an expedition to West Africa for seven years. We still cannot be exactly sure why.

Some say that it was because once again the navigator had become deeply involved in the affairs of the realm. This was certainly true, for civil war now threatened Portugal. In 1447, although King Affonso was only fifteen years old, Dom Pedro resigned the office of regent. He hoped to return to the peace of his books and his acres near the beautiful city of Coimbra.

He did, but unfortunately he was not to stay for long. No sooner had he left his nephew, than his half brother, the Count of Barcelos, moved in and set out to poison Affonso's mind.

"Pedro is not really laying down the regency," he told the young king. "He is only pretending to lay it down. The reason he has retired to his estates in the country is so that he can raise an army with which to overthrow you and become king in your stead."

After a year of such talk, Affonso allowed himself to be

convinced, and sent his unhappy wife—she was Dom Pedro's daughter—to offer her father a hard choice.

"Either death, or life imprisonment, or exile is my husband's message to you!"

"I choose death!" Dom Pedro told his daughter.

Then, surrounded by his followers, he marched from Coimbra to Santarém, where the king was supposed to be. In front of him two banners were borne. One of them was inscribed *Justice and Vengeance*, but the other was emblazoned with the one word, *Loyalty*. Those who knew Pedro say that the second banner expressed his true feelings. It was his intention, they say, to fall on his knees before his royal nephew, and after reminding him of his long service, swear that it would continue as long as he lived.

Be that as it may, he never had the chance. For the king marched out to meet him, and as the two armies approached, some royal archers, ambushed in a nearby wood, began to shoot. In reply, Pedro ordered a bombard to be discharged. The aim was bad and its heavy stone missile fell near Affonso's tent.

Shaken with anger and fear, the king ordered his guards to charge, and a savage battle broke out. It did not last for long, however, for the royal archers also kept up their withering attack. And Dom Pedro, who had rushed into the melee only lightly armed, was pierced through the heart by a random arrow. At his side fell Alvaro Vaz de Almada, regarded as the noblest knight in Portugal since Nun'Álvares. With that, all resistance crumbled. The king's victory was complete.

Henry's admirers insist that he tried to prevent this tragic happening, and we do know that as soon as he learned that trouble was brewing, he galloped north, supposedly to persuade his nephew not to listen to evil councilors. However, his critics have another theory. Their version is that Affonso bribed Henry to remain neutral. The battle in which Pedro was slain, they point out, was fought on May 5, 1449, but as far back as September 15, 1447, the young king had made a bid for Henry's good will by not even trying to oppose Pedro's decree—it was made in his name—that no ship could sail past Cape Bojador without Henry's permission. Once again, they ask, did his African adventures mean more to him than a brother?

Another reason given for Henry's failure to send his ships to Africa for seven years is that he was now more concerned with the Canary Islands. There is no doubt that the Canaries were much on his mind. And why not? Although they had been granted to Castile by more than one pope, didn't they lie right on the flank of his African discoveries? Wouldn't they provide useful bases for his vessels sailing there?

We know, too, that Portuguese expeditions did go out against these islands in 1450, 1451, and 1453, and it is hard to believe that they would have dared do this without Henry's encouragement. And were Henry sending fleets—even small fleets—to the Canaries, he could surely not have sent fleets to West Africa at the same time.

A third reason for Henry's not sending his vessels toward the Sénégal and the Gambia could have been that he was now looking in another direction; that he was now looking farther west and south. Some even say that his captains were sailing thither, that Henry's seamen actually reached South America and the West Indies and the Grand Banks of Newfoundland during his lifetime.

The majority of the scholars who have studied the matter do not think so, and they give good reasons for reaching this conclusion. The most convincing one: How could such discoveries have been kept secret?

But there are some arguments on the other side of the question, and these arguments have supporters too.

A Portuguese historian, writing a hundred years later, says that "about this time [1447] a Portuguese ship coming out of the Straits of Gibraltar was carried westward farther than was intended and came to an island on which there were seven cities. The people there spoke our language and some say that it was part of what the Spaniards now call the Antilles." Even the historian found this hard to believe—especially that the people on the island spoke Portuguese. It is not impossible that a Portuguese ship did reach the Caribbean, although more probably the captain merely wanted to come home with a tall tale. In order to do so he may have revived the widespread medieval legend that when the Moors took over the Spanish peninsula in the eighth century the Bishop of Lisbon sailed with a band of followers to an island far in the western ocean and there built seven cities.

A map published in 1448 had on it a long stretch of land some two hundred miles southwest of Cape Verde. This was inscribed "authentic island about fifteen hundred miles to the west." Many think that this was part of the coast of South America.

In 1457, and again in 1462, King Affonso granted to his nephew Fernando "an island west northwest of the Canaries and Madeira," which was said to have been discovered by a Portuguese captain returning from the Río de Oro.

Another Portuguese mariner insisted that around 1450 he had sailed northwest until he had come to shallow waters teeming with cod, but that he was driven back by cold weather and dense fog. This sounds very much like the shoal waters of Nova Scotia and Newfoundland.

Besides that, recall the course sailed by Vasco da Gama. Remember that when he set out for India, he sailed almost to Brazil to find the fair winds that would take him to the Cape of Good Hope. Was this just blind luck or did someone who had been to Brazil or near it instruct him?

We may never know the true story. Henry's records—those that had not already been scattered—were almost all destroyed when the English, under Sir Francis Drake, sacked Sagres in 1587, and most other Portuguese records perished in the great Lisbon earthquake of 1755.

Finally, Henry may have been held back because he was short of money. He had enormous resources—not only the revenues of the Order of Christ, but the large grants made to him annually by the crown—yet when he died he left debts of more than half a million dollars. It is possible that for a while he simply could not afford to send out ships. The expenses were great, and the profits, if any, were small.

But probably the most important reason why Henry's voyages did not continue was that he could no longer find the kind of captains he wanted. Gone were the days when an Alvaro de Freitas could cry to his men: "I say let us press on even to the Earthly Paradise!" Gone were the days of Gil Eannes and Nuno Tristão.

Now, for the most part, Henry's seafarers did not wish to fare farther than the Río de Oro or Arguin Bay. In both places, they could do business safely with people who knew their ways, and on Arguin Island there was even a mud-and-stone fort to protect them. They were now merchants, not adventurers. What Henry wanted was adventurers—they could be merchants too—who had some of the zest and spirit of his earlier men.

He found one, but he was not Portuguese.

Alvise Cadamosto was a Venetian. He was between twenty-two and twenty-five, good-looking, and as a member of one of the oldest and noblest families in Venice (their home, the Cá da Mosto, is still one of the most beautiful palaces on the Grand Canal), he had been born into luxury and wealth.

But when he was still hardly more than a boy, the Cadamosti had fallen into difficult days, and like many another noble young Venetian, Alvise had to make his own fortune all over again. This he did by becoming a trader. Before he was twenty, he had made profitable voyages to Tunis and Alexandria—but always in someone else's employ. He soon learned that the only way to amass wealth was to be on one's own, so in 1454 he got together "such small moneys as [he] then had" and invested them in the Flanders venture of a fleet commanded by one Marco Zeno, "who had had much experience in the business." On one of its galleys, he set sail for Bruges between August 8 and August 11.

He got little farther than the Straits of Gibraltar. For just as the vessels were pushing out into the Atlantic, a storm came sweeping in and they had to take refuge in the lee of Cape St. Vincent. There, very shortly, they had visitors: Patrizio Conti, who said that he was the Venetian consul, and Henry's secretary, Antão Gonçalves, the one who had helped capture Adahu.

Henry had sent them, they told the Venetians, and evidently to arouse their interest, for they brought with them samples of "the various fine things which came from the lands and islands subject to the above prince." Madeira sugar, for example. And dragon's blood, which was the red resin of a tropical tree used in making dye.

"But where are these lands and islands?" asked Cadamosto.

"Far away, and reached only by sailing seas that no one has ever sailed before, and peopled by men of unknown races. Yet you can make great profit there, since for each *soldo* you invest you will earn between seven and ten."

"But can anyone sail there? Anyone who wishes to?"

"He can indeed," replied Antão, and Patrizio Conti echoed him. "That is, if he agrees to Prince Henry's conditions."

"What are these conditions?"

"If you fit out a vessel yourself, and at your own expense put aboard it all the merchandise you need, three fourths the profits are yours and the remaining quarter is Henry's. If he fits out the vessel and you only put on the goods, he keeps half the profit, you the other half. But if the vessel is lost and your cargo with it, he reimburses you."

"It seems good," said Cadamosto. "May I hear it from the prince?"

"You may," replied Antão and took him to his master.

There Henry confirmed all that Antão had said and added that he was particularly glad to have a Venetian serving him, since the Venetians were the ones who really knew the spice trade—the spice trade which would be so important when the Portuguese reached India. Henry must have thought that they were nearing it!

Cadamosto thereupon returned to his galley and placed all his Flanders business in the hands of a cousin who was aboard her. He also bought from her cargo the things he would need for his voyage.

"I am leaving you to sail for Guinea," he told his former shipmates.

"Why?" they asked him. *"Why?"*

"Because I am young and can endure hardships," was Cadamosto's answer. "Because I want to see the world and those things in it no one of my race (no Venetian, no Italian even) has ever looked upon. But also because I wish glory as well as profit."

He spent the winter at Sagres, learning all he could from Henry and supervising the construction of a ninety-ton caravel the prince was having built for him. Aboard it, he set sail on March 22, 1455. He reached Porto Santo on March 25 and Madeira on March 27.

From the latter—to Henry's delight—he sent back the kind of report to be expected from a merchant of Venice who from boyhood had learned how to balance books.

"The island," he said, "has only been inhabited for twenty-four years"—actually it had been inhabited for more than thirty years—"and already there are eight hundred inhabitants dwelling in four towns. Although mountainous, it is very fertile. It produces thirty thousand Venetian bushels of wheat annually, and the soil still yields from thirty- to forty-fold. In the beginning, the yield was sixty- to seventy-fold. There is a flourishing saw-mill industry, the principal woods being a sort of cedar that resembles cypress, and a very handsome red-hearted yew. Sugar growers prosper, for the cane imported from Sicily does so well that more than five thousand quarts are often made from a single boiling. A little honey is produced, and although the vines imported from Crete were relatively new, the wine is so good that there are few places in the world which do not buy it. There are plenty of cattle."

There was even game—wild boar, wild peacocks, wild guinea fowl, pheasants and quail, as well as wild pigeons which were so tame that they could be pulled from the trees with a lasso. The desert island was a desert island no more.

From Madeira, Cadamosto went on toward the Canaries, and presently he saw the twelve-thousand-foot-high, snow-crowned peak of Teyde. This peak was on Tenerife, the largest island of the group, and "sea captains worthy of belief" had told the Venetian that when conditions were favorable, it could be seen "when it was two hundred and fifty miles away." Although there were a few small European settlements on four of the islands, Cadamosto did not find a little Portugal like Madeira or even a little Spain in the Canaries. Instead, most of the islands were inhabited by primitive aborigines, the Guanche, who were naked except for small goatskins which hung from their waists. The Guanche spoke a language like none other in the world, and stained themselves red or green or yellow, just as the ancient Britons dyed their skin blue with woad.

The Canaries had neither wine nor wheat except when it was imported. The inhabitants lived on barley bread, goat meat, goat milk, figs, and a crude cheese. They did not use iron, but fought with stones or with fire-hardened wooden javelins or with clubs. Some of their customs were barbarous. For instance, when a new chief was chosen, one of his subjects voluntarily leaped to death over a high cliff to celebrate the occasion. The chief then had to honor and support the man's family. They were pagans, worshipping the sun, the moon, or one of the planets. They were polygamous. A Guanche could have as many wives as he wished.

"All this," said Cadamosto, "I learned from slaves, for I only went ashore on those islands that had Christian settlements."

In view of the fact that the Guanche did not kill their prisoners but enslaved them and set them to revolting tasks, it is hard to blame him.

After he left the Canaries, Cadamosto sailed to Cape Blanc over open ocean, and then into the Bay of Arguin. There he landed, and did something that only João Fernandes had done before him. He made a camel-back journey inland. (To be sure, his lasted only six days, not seven months, but he did leave the safety of his ship.) He went to a place called Oden (now Oudane in present day Mauritania) where traders came in laden with copper and silver and left carrying gold and malaguete pepper from Timbuktu and elsewhere.

At Oden, Cadamosto learned very few things that João had not learned before him, but what he did learn he reported in great detail. The white-robed Oden Assenegs particularly wanted to buy cotton and linen cloth, silver ingots, silken scarves, tapestry, and wheat. They wanted the latter, Cadamosto noted, because "they were always hungry." This is not surprising. Not only was their land almost entirely dry desert, but every three or four years a horde of red locusts descended on them, darkening the skies and eating everything in sight. Sometimes the horde covered an area of almost two hundred square miles. Relief came only when the harmattan blew them to sea.

The inland Assenegs, Cadamosto continued, had no money, but many of them used cowrie shells instead. (This was important for Henry and his captains to know, for they had now been trading with the coastal Assenegs for at least a decade, and they wished to extend this trade toward the interior.) They had no hereditary chiefs. They respected the rich only— those who had a few cattle and a few horses and many camels. Almost all of them were rogues and thieves, yet no one surpassed them in hospitality. Even when they were starving, they allowed no stranger to go without food.

Some of their personal habits, said Cadamosto, were far from attractive. They let their thick black hair grow long, and once a day they anointed it with foul-smelling fish oil. It was not pleasant to come near a well-groomed Asseneg. Lean though they were, they liked their women—who were much darker than the men—to be fat. Some of them were repulsively so. As for their clothing, the Assenegs felt that they were decently clad so long as they were garbed from the waist down and the mouth was covered (they regarded the mouth as unclean, and men and women alike always hid it behind a veil).

From the Bay of Arguin and its Assenegs, Cadamosto went on to the Sénégal River. He traveled it for sixty miles, thus becoming the first European to take a ship deep into the heart of Africa. Here he found a new kind of people.

"Beyond the Sénégal, there are no more Assenegs," he reported to Henry, "and instead of these Berretini (tawny desert people), we found the true blacks. The latter are tall and have the build of athletes. They live in a beautiful land of huge trees and strange, delicious fruit." (Another explorer had observed that even a few miles offshore the air was fragrant.) "They call themselves Jaloffs, and along the coast at least, they are ruled by a young man named Zucolin. But he does not rule for life. Only so long as his people are satisfied with him."

A black himself, Zucolin nevertheless had his own black slaves, who tilled the soil for him. He was allowed thirty wives. These he scattered about here and there in the various villages of his realm, and it was their duty to provide him with food and entertainment. When the food in one village was used up, he moved on to another village and another wife.

The Jaloffs were Moslems, but they were not fanatical Moslems as the Assenegs were.

"God must love the Christians, too," one of them told Cadamosto. "Otherwise He would not have made them so rich and powerful."

In contrast to the Assenegs, the Jaloffs were very cleanly. The women bathed as often as four or five times a day and some of the men did too. Like the Assenegs, however, they were clothed from the waist down only, either in goatskins or in cotton. The cotton was woven at home, and by men as well as women. They did not wear armor—the climate was too hot—but some of the Jaloffs had Moorish scimitars, and they knew and used crude iron. Surprisingly, Cadamosto indicated, it did not come from the north and the Arabs, "but was smelted somewhere in the Gambia country farther south."

Having explored the Sénégal and learned all he needed to, Cadamosto pushed on toward Cape Verde. Near it, he came upon a second black kingdom, the land of Budomel, called this after Budomel (Bor Damel, or King Damel), who ruled it.

And now Cadamosto really established contact with black Africa. Upon learning that Budomel coveted horses above everything else in the world, he sent ashore an interpreter with an offer of seven spirited Arab steeds and three hundred ducats worth of European linen, Moorish silk, and various other goods. In answer, Budomel sent a mounted escort of thirteen horsemen, and one hundred and fifty assagai-carrying foot soldiers.

"Come to my house," he said, "and for your seven horses I will give you one hundred strong and healthy slaves. I will throw in a beautiful slave girl for yourself."

Cadamosto accepted.

"I went," he told Henry later, "fully as much to see and hear as to receive any payment."

See and hear the young Venetian surely did. Budomel's village—his capital if you could call it that—was twenty-five miles inland and Cadamosto was escorted there by Budomel's nephew, Bisborer. He stayed there for twenty-eight days.

To one who knew the great cities of Italy and Egypt, it was not much of a place, for it was little more than a collection of forty-five or fifty oval straw huts surrounded by a palisade made of felled tree trunks and having at most two or three entrances or gates.

But here, surrounded by a personal retinue that never numbered fewer than two hundred, Budomel lived amid a pomp and circumstance that would have satisfied many another absolute monarch. His residence was surrounded by seven courtyards. In the center of each was a tree. In the shade of these trees, and arranged according to rank, waited those who wished to petition him. They shook with fear and apprehension. Twice a day, a signal was given, and one at a time, they filed into the royal presence.

But they did not walk toward their monarch. No matter what his rank, anyone who was granted an audience had to crawl up to Budomel on his knees, clad only in a loincloth, and casting dirt or dust upon his head. Then he humbly voiced his request, but Budomel acted as if he had not heard it. He looked absently into the air and then spoke, as an afterthought, to an attendant. When he did this, he never used more than two or three words, but these held life or death.

"I do not think God himself could have been accorded greater reverence," said Cadamosto.

It was only his own subjects, however, that Budomel treated in this manner. He permitted Asseneg missionaries to approach him without formality, and he allowed Cadamosto to do the same. He even invited Cadamosto to watch him at his prayers and then urged him to discuss religion with him.

"The Moslem and the Christian religions are both good," Budomel said, "but I think that we blacks have a better chance for salvation than either of you." The reason: "God is just, and since you have your paradise here, we will have it in the world to come."

Cadamosto saw more than the tall and white-plumed ruler, however, and this too he reported. There was no wheat, barley, or spelt in Budomel's domain. There were no vines. But there was millet and the finest beans Cadamosto had ever seen, some as large as hazelnuts and spotted all over, others either rose-colored or white. Budomel's subjects drank water, milk, and palm wine. The latter was good to the taste and very strong. For oil, they used palm oil, which was similar to olive oil. It smelled like violets and was of a beautiful yellow color.

The climate was hard on domestic animals. Oxen, cows, and goats could survive after a fashion, but not sheep, and horses did not live long. That is why they were so highly valued. However, the jungle abounded with wild animals, among them lions, leopards, and wild goats.

"I also saw wild elephants. They roved through the undergrowth in great herds as swine do with us. I will not tell you of their size nor of their long tusks, for this you know about, but it is not true that they cannot kneel."

Cadamosto was taken to an African fair. These were held once a week—"on either a Monday or a Friday." Here five thousand men and women came swarming in to sell cotton, vegetables, honey, oil, wooden bowls, and palm mats. But not the gold he was seeking.

"They also came to see me. They marveled at my Spanish-style clothes—at my black damask shirt and my gray woolen mantle. They also marveled at my white skin. Some of them wet their fingers and tried to rub off what they thought must be dye."

In return, Cadamosto entertained Budomel and his "lords" aboard his ship. He covered a table with white linen, set out his best silver and pewter service, and spread on it boiled and roasted meat, broiled, boiled, and fried fish, wine, and sweet-meats made of almonds and sugar. Around it he arranged chairs, and then invited his guests to partake of the meal. This they did with great gusto, but they refused to sit in the chairs. It was their custom to eat sitting on the ground.

An inspection of the ship followed, and the African king and those with him looked with amazement at masts as tall as trees, sails as large as the floor of Budomel's dwelling, and the tremendous anchor. They wondered if the eyes on the bow of the caravel—painted there to ward off evil spirits—were real eyes by which the ship could see its way across the ocean. They fell prostrate on the deck when a bombard was discharged. It seemed to them that the Portuguese commanded the lightning and the thunder.

Strangely enough, what impressed them most was a berib-boned bagpipe played by one of the sailors. "They thought that it was some kind of animal," said Cadamosto, "or that it was the work of a sorcerer, but when they found that it was neither, everyone wanted to have one."

After this banquet, Cadamosto went ashore again, bought some slaves, and then decided it was time to continue on his travels. But when he reached the beach, the West African surf had begun to roar and it was too rough for him to be rowed to his ship. Some of Budomel's men had accompanied him this far, and he offered a pewter jug to any one of them who would swim through the wild welter—the vessel lay three miles offshore—and carry a message to the captain, directing him to meet the explorer at the mouth of the Sénégal, where the water would be smoother. He would proceed there overland. To his surprise, two men volunteered and one of them made it. "I can only say," was Cadamosto's comment, "that I have never seen so great a swimmer in the whole world."

From the Sénégal, Cadamosto turned again toward the south. But no longer was he alone, for hardly was he under way when two other caravels came into sight. One was commanded by "another of Henry's squires," and the second by Antoniotto Usodimare—his name was a nickname; the English equivalent would be Tony Seadog—whom Cadamosto described as "a Genoese gentleman and a great navigator."

Antoniotto suggested that they join forces and, this seeming good to Cadamosto, the three ships proceeded in company —past Cape Verde, carefully making sure that they cleared the rocky reefs which extend at least a mile seaward, and then pausing at an unnamed island (probably Gorée near Dakar) to fish for dentex and dorados. (These fishes were familiar to all who had sailed the Mediterranean, but their size was not. "Although it was only June," said Cadamosto, "some of them weighed fifteen pounds!")

They sailed along a low green shore where the jungle came to within a bowshot of the sea, and passed the mouths of many small rivers and little streams where, hidden in the bush, they could see clusters of reed and seaweed huts. Now they sailed only by day, anchoring at night four or five miles offshore in ten to twelve fathoms.

Finally they came to a river sixty miles south of Cape Verde and "as large as the Sénégal." This may have been the Saloum. Here they had their only serious misadventure. Feeling that he was now nearing the true "River of Gold," Cadamosto put ashore one of his dragomen—Negro slaves who could win their freedom (and four slaves of their own) if they served the Portuguese by acting as interpreters—to make inquiries. The slave was rowed to the shore, where he leaped from the boat and walked slowly up the beach, looking for some sign of life. Suddenly a band of armed blacks burst from the underbrush and surrounded him. They talked to him with animation for a long while—no one knows what they said—and then without warning, turned upon him and cut him to pieces.

"We were dumbstruck," said Cadamosto, "but we knew that if they treated one of their own people in this way, they would deal the same with us, and so we sailed on."

But not for long. Heading southwestward now, they came very shortly to still another great river seven or eight miles wide and deep enough for the caravels to sail up as many miles as their captain wished. This must indeed have been the Gambia. Supposedly the fabled city of Cantor lay far up this river. Legend had it that Cantor was no straw-hut village like Budomel's, but a walled city (even if the walls may not have been of stone) where gold from the other side of Sierra Leone started on its long journey to Timbuktu, and then to Carthage, Tunis, Fez, and Cairo.

Obviously, Cadamosto must try to go to Cantor, and he sent the smallest caravel up the river, sounding and poling. The ship's boats followed and then the other caravels. But as they reached a point where a small tributary flowed into the main stream, first three canoes carrying twenty-five or thirty blacks, and then a flotilla of seventeen with at least one hundred and fifty warriors armed with bows and poisoned arrows came sweeping toward them. They were only dispersed when a shot from one of the bombards fell into their midst.

Cadamosto had not come to fight, however, and he managed to persuade the men in one canoe to approach him.

"I am here to trade," he cried. "I have been sent by the King of Portugal to trade and be friendly."

"Trade?" answered one of the black leaders. "And be friendly? But we know what you come to trade for. You come to take prisoners and then eat them. We have learned this from our brothers of the Sénégal."

Cadamosto now faced a difficult choice; he must either push his way onward and risk ambush at every bend and turn, or return to Portugal and report his disappointment to Henry.

His crew decided for him.

"We have gone far enough and endured enough for one voyage. It is time for us to go home now."

He gave in to them. He had to. Down the river he went, pausing only to jot down in his notebooks a few more of his careful observations. For instance, in this latitude the day in July was thirteen hours long, the night eleven. There was no twilight in tropical Africa. It was broad day and then it was pitch black. He also noted that there was now a new and beautiful constellation in the heavens. It was made up of six large, clear stars arranged in the shape of a cross, and as the North Star sank to the height of a man above the horizon it dazzled the eyes.

"I called it the Southern Chariot," said Cadamosto. It was in fact the Southern Cross.

In many ways, Cadamosto's second voyage, which took place in 1456, was a repetition of the first. Again, there were three caravels, and again Antoniotto Usodimare commanded one of them. This time, however, Cadamosto sailed directly from Lagos to Cape Blanc under skies that grew warmer every day, and this time he was able to sail up the Gambia, for the blacks now welcomed him. Indeed, a party of them waited for him by the river mouth and they did not carry drawn bows and deadly arrows.

"The stories we were told about you were lies," said their leader, a tall man clad in white cotton. "We wish to buy with you and sell with you."

"Who wishes to do this?" asked Cadamosto.

"Our ruler, Battimansa."

Then they explained how—or how they thought—black Africa was governed. Ruler of all, they said, was the distant ruler of Melli, who protected them from the Assenegs and other nomads, but under him, and ruling most of the lands south of the Sénégal, was one Farosangoli, who lived ten days' journey away. Farosangoli had his own vassal kings. One of them was Battimansa, who lived sixty miles up the river and would be glad to have Cadamosto visit him.

With this encouragement, Cadamosto forthwith sent another of his dragomen to the jungle king with an *alcimba* (Moorish robe) of elaborately embroidered silk and other peace offerings. He himself followed in his caravel.

Cadamosto stayed with Battimansa only two days, but even in that short time he was able to do considerable business. Battimansa gave him gold, which the African considered a trifle, civet (a yellowish substance used in making perfumes), civet cats, baboons, marmots, and cotton garments ("not only white," said Cadamosto, "but green; blue and white; white, blue, and red; and they were very well made"). All this was exchanged for trinkets that the Portuguese thought were trifles.

Then, because one after another his men began to fall ill with high fevers that came suddenly and were unshakable, Cadamosto turned downstream again.

When he reached the sea, he did not immediately head north. Hugging the coast as closely as he dared, and for the first time carefully trying to note and remember its many reefs and shoals, he continued south until he came to the Cattimansa River; then to Cape Roxo (which he named); then to two small rivers, the Rio de Santa Anna (now the Cacheu) and the São Domingo (now the Mansôa); and finally to another great river which was probably the Geba.

"It was so wide that it was almost a gulf," said Cadamosto, "and while there I noted a strange phenomenon. Unlike Venice and other seaports in the west where the tide floods for six hours and then ebbs for six, the tide in this river floods for four hours and then ebbs for eight." (This, of course, was because so much water came down the river that it held back the flood tide for a while. The same thing happens in other great rivers.) "And the current was so swift at its height, that three anchors would not hold my vessel."

This was the farthest that any of Henry's captains except Alvaro Fernandes had gone as yet, and Alvaro did not make the careful observations Cadamosto did. (A little later, one of Henry's captains did sail farther. Pedro de Cintra went at least as far as Sierra Leone, so named because the grumbling thunder around its mountains sounded like lions roaring. He may even have reached the Gold Coast. But although Pedro's expedition was organized by Henry, it did not take place until after his death.)

After reaching the mouth of the Geba, Cadamosto returned to Portugal, again with a full cargo of stories. One of the most exciting was about an elephant hunt in which he had evidently taken part. The great beasts were driven in a wild stampede toward trees in whose branches hunters lay hidden. From this vantage point, they brought their quarry down with poisoned arrows or poisoned assagais. Sometimes a hunter tumbled to the ground. Then the elephant seized him in its trunk and hurled him to his death.

Cadamosto spoke of another great animal, "the horsefish"— that is, the hippopotamus.

He told of what he called the people's "devil worship." He had witnessed some of the wild dances associated with it.

He also reported the discovery of another island group. After the three vessels passed Cape Blanc on their way southward, his and Antoniotto's were driven southwestward by a gale for three days and two nights until they came to land no one had seen before. It turned out to be an island surrounded by other islands. He went ashore and found a deep river, much unbelievably white salt, thousands of doves, and innumerable huge sea turtles. He named it São Jácome. We know now that it was one of the Cape Verdes. It and the surrounding islands, all of them volcanic, were bare, brown, and compared to the Azores, Madeira, and the Canaries, unappealing. But in due course, they became important to the Portuguese empire, for after South America was discovered, and until the advent of steamships ended the age of the sail, they were an important way station on the road to Brazil.

Cadamosto's two voyages were not quite the last made in Henry's lifetime by one of the prince's captains.

When Nuno Tristão took the first caravel to Africa in 1441, one of his lieutenants was a certain Gomes Vinagre (Gomes Vinegar), called this because of his sour disposition. His real name was Diogo Gomes, and now, seventeen years later, he was an explorer and discoverer in his own right.

We know that he sailed after Cadamosto and before Henry's death, but it is difficult to be certain just where he went and what he did. All we have to go on is the Latin version of Gomes's own account, which he gave to the German geographer Martin Behaim (Martin of Bohemia) when he was more than eighty years old. It seems likely that this account at least partly reflects the imaginings of an old man whose memory was confused and who liked to boast. For instance, everything that Cadamosto wanted to do and didn't, Gomes says he did.

Cadamosto wished to establish a real and profitable trade with the blacks. Gomes says he himself did. He established relations, he says, with Farangsick, who was a nephew of Cadamosto's Farosangoli, and instead of civet cats and cotton was given 180 pounds of gold. Another chief, he claims, gave him so many "elephant's teeth" that it took four slaves to carry them. Cadamosto wanted to go to Cantor. Again Gomes says he went there. To be sure, he did not find it as splendid as he expected. There was gold at Cantor but most of it came from either the mines of "some mountains to the south" or Kukia. Kukia was a "great city surrounded by walls of baked tile" and there was an abundance of gold there. A block of it before the king's palace was so heavy it took twenty men to move it. The king tethered his horse to it. The nobles of his court wore gold ornaments in their noses and ears.

Gomes also says he converted a great chief, Nomimansa, to Christianity. (*Mansa* seems to be another name for chief or king. There was a Batti*mansa*, a Cassa*mansa*, and an Olli-*mansa*.) Nomimansa wanted Gomes to baptize him and when the latter replied that he could not do this because he was not a priest, Nomimansa begged Gomes to have Henry send him one, and also "one of those birds that hunt from a man's hand [he meant a falcon, of course]," a ram and a ewe, a gander and a goose, and some pigs. The most Cadamosto had done was to persuade Budomel and Battimansa to agree that Christianity was a good religion.

Finally, he, and he only, Gomes claims, discovered the Cape Verde Islands—this despite the fact that they were already on Portuguese maps.

"On the way home from the Gambia," he tells Behaim, "I and Antonio da Noli"—this was not Antoniotto Usodimare as was once believed—"had sailed for two days and a night when we sighted islands far out in the ocean. We sailed toward them but my ship was the faster so I came to them first and anchored off one of them. I called it São Tiago. But Antonio reached Portugal before me, and he got the credit."

And besides this, says Gomes in a final story, "I was quick thinking and clever enough to outwit one of the most dangerous and most hostile of the West African chiefs." His name was Beziguichi, and he ruled a long strip of coast near Cape Verde. As Gomes cruised there one day, canoes approached him, and his interpreter told him that Beziguichi was aboard one of them. Gomes hailed them and invited the men onto his caravel. There he questioned the one he had been told was Beziguichi.

"Is this the land of Beziguichi?"

"It is," said Beziguichi.

"Why does this man hate us so? Why does he always make war upon us Christians? We only want to trade with him, and in proof of this take him this message. Tell him that we had you on our ship and could have kept you there, but for our love of him, we did not. Now get you back into your canoes and go to him."

They did, but as they paddled off and were still in hearing Gomes shouted to them.

"Beziguichi!" he cried. "Beziguichi! I know you. You were my prisoner but I let you go. See that from henceforward you are friend, not enemy."

Many of the things Diogo Gomes narrates are, you will surely agree, hard to believe. But the fact is that he *did* sail for Africa and that he did at least *some* of the things he said he had done. And if he dressed up his stories a little or even a lot, it is hardly surprising. After all, he was a seaman. Why shouldn't he spin seamen's yarns?

The Last Adventure

When Diogo Gomes set out for Africa, Henry was sixty-four, and although in some ways he was as full of vigor as ever, he was beginning to feel his years. However, he still had one more adventure ahead of him—an adventure touched off by an event at the other end of Europe. He plunged into it heart and soul.

On May 29, 1453, Constantinople fell to the Turks, and a shock wave raced westward like a tidal bore. Was history going to repeat itself? Between A.D. 632 and 732 the Moslem Arabs had fought their way from Arabia to the heart of medieval France. They still held parts of southern Spain. Would these new Moslems move into eastern and southern Europe? Would they even raise the star and crescent over St. Peter's?

The Pope—Calixtus III, a Spaniard and the first Borgia—was afraid they would. He promptly proclaimed a crusade. Only Portugal responded. From England, busy fighting the first of the Wars of the Roses, to distant Scandinavia, all powers were occupied with their own problems. Even in threatened Italy an observer could find neither "the preparations nor the desire needed for such an enterprise."

But in Portugal young King Affonso burned with chivalrous zeal. He would be a knight as his uncles and his father had been before him. Over the protests of his subjects, he issued a new gold coin, the *cruzado*, and set about raising an army of twelve thousand men and assembling the ships to transport it.

Then Pope Calixtus died, and the whole enterprise fell through. What should Affonso do?

A suggestion soon came: Why not send the army to North Africa instead? The idea was greeted with enthusiasm, especially by Henry.

"It is near," he told his nephew. "It is not thousands of miles away, but even from Sagres, less than two hundred. It is easy to reach too, and we know the coast well. An expedition there would be cheaper than a crusade. For the cost of moving twelve thousand men to the Bosporus you could send four-and-twenty thousand men, and you could equip two hundred ships instead of one hundred. It would serve Christianity just as well—the Moors are Moslems just as the Turks are. It would avenge Prince Fernando. And it would also serve Portugal."

"But where in North Africa?" asked Affonso.

"Not Tangier," Henry replied, for he knew that Affonso, who loved glory, was thinking of Tangier. "Tangier would be too difficult, as I know only too well. Alcácer Ceguer."

"Alcácer Ceguer?"

"It is a small town on the Atlantic seacoast. Small and lightly defended, and since it lies outside the straits, you would not have to pass through their narrow waters. But it is important, for it outflanks the mountains and the other Moorish cities. If you take it, Tangier will one day fall to you like a ripe Moroccan plum. One day, when the time comes. Not tomorrow. In a year. In twenty years. One day."

"Alcácer? Good. Let it be Alcácer," said Affonso.

He ordered the expedition to set out.

This it did—and with very little delay. Affonso departed from Setúbal on September 30, 1458, and reached Sagres on October 3. There Henry awaited him with more vessels and "a very perfect speech." It is not hard to imagine it. Two weeks were then spent in further preparations, and on October 17 the armada set sail, heading southeastward. Two hundred and eighty vessels—that was the final number—and half of them flaunting on their sails the red cross of Henry's Order of Christ. It reached Tangier on October 19 but only to pause for a day until a fair wind blew. It reached Alcácer Ceguer on October 21, and the siege began.

In many ways, it was Ceuta all over again. At midnight the city was bombarded heavily. Henry himself fired the first shot. It went straight to its target and a section of the white walls crumbled. Then at dawn, the Portuguese landed, and after a sharp struggle, forced the defenders back into the city.

"The Infante," cried one of Henry's admirers, "led the troops in this assault—and with something of his youthful fire!"

It was Henry, too, who inspired his men to great deeds of valor as the Portuguese moved up their bombards, military engines and scaling ladders in the face of gunfire, crossbow bolts, and a barrage of heavy stones, and it was he who accepted the city's surrender when the Moors finally gave in.

"What are your terms?" he was asked.

"That you yield the city to us and leave behind you all your Christian slaves. The rest of your property you can take with you, and your wives and children too."

"Give us time to consider," they begged him.

"Two days," he replied. "Two days and two days only."

But the defenders did not wait for two days. Henry had made it plain that his conditions would not be modified by even a comma, and that if they were not accepted he would sack the place and massacre every last man, woman, and child. So on October 23, a long column accompanied by heavily laden mules and camels marched out in good order in the direction of Fez. When at last it had vanished, Affonso entered the place. He was accompanied by Henry, by his own brother, Fernando, and by his cousin, Prince Pedro, son of the regent Pedro. In a mosque which had already been rededicated as the Church of St. Mary, they celebrated a solemn mass of victory. It was the first important victory that the Portuguese had celebrated in forty-three years.

It was also Henry's last official public appearance. He remained in Africa for only a few weeks longer. He showed Affonso how to organize the defense of Alcácer, which he predicted the Moors would soon attempt to retake. (They did, but so well had the defenses been planned that the governor—he was the son of the old governor of Ceuta—was able to hold out although the King of Fez with 100,000 men beseiged the city for fifty-three days.)

Henry took the young king to Ceuta. Affonso had never seen Ceuta before and he was so dazzled by its splendor that then and there he decided on a career of conquest that would win him not only Tangier but Casablanca too, and the title of Affonso the African.

Soon after, on a wild November day of rain and driving mist, Henry returned to Portugal. As spray leaped mast-high over his lurching vessel, he looked back over the stern at the slowly disappearing white peaks of the Atlas Mountains. Finally, he could see them no more; nor would he ever see Africa again. Soon Henry was at Sagres and at Sagres he remained for what was left of his life.

There, almost as if sensing that the end approached, he set to work putting his affairs in order. He assembled his papers and reports—all the mass of information that his sea captains and his mariners had gathered and brought back, and he made arrangements for them to be kept available for those who needed them.

He did the same with his maps and his charts, and saw to it too that the great world map he was having drawn for him in Italy was completed. Andrea Bianco and Fra Mauro were the mapmakers (they were perhaps the two greatest of the age), and to insure privacy the drafting was done on the little island of Murano near Venice.

"When will it be done?" Henry asked Doge Francesco Foscari anxiously, for the two men were making it under Foscari's orders at the request of King Affonso.

"It is done already," answered Foscari, "and a copy will shortly be sent to you. I hope that Your Excellency will find in it further inducements to carry on your explorations."

When the map arrived, Henry gazed at it with admiration. Not only was it "the masterpiece of medieval cartography and the most beautiful map in the world"; it was also one of the most remarkable, for in their own way, the men who drew it were as adventurous as Henry. They refused to be bound by out-of-date ideas, and among other things, discarded the long-held theory that the Indian Ocean was landlocked. Instead of stretching Africa eastward until it joined the Malay Peninsula, they made the African continent end in a triangular cape, which they labeled Diab. As proof, they set down a story they had heard of men who had sailed around it.

"About the year of our Lord 1420, an Indian junk (*zoncho de India*)," reads an inscription on the map, "sailed westward from the Indian Sea past Cape Diab toward the Sea of Darkness in the direction of the Algarve. Nothing but air and water were seen for forty days."

What did this mean? Had someone already done what

Henry hoped to do—but in the opposite direction? Had he known it before he saw the map? If so, had this knowledge given him the courage to send his men on?

Henry also discussed plans for the future with some of his captains—with Pedro de Cintra, who actually did sail to Africa after Henry's death, and with Diogo Gomes (we have already read his account of his first voyage), who wanted to go to Africa for a second time.

Gomes said that he must go to fulfill a pledge he had made. "I promised Nomimansa," he said, "that you would send a priest to him. When he is baptized he will take the name of Henry."

Henry made arrangements for Gomes to do this. He summoned a learned churchman into his presence and directed him to make ready to go with his captain.

"You will go with Gomes," he said, and when you are there, he will take you to Nomimansa. You will remain with him and instruct him in the faith."

He also commanded a young squire, João Delgado, to accompany the party.

"It will be your task," he told João, "to teach Nomimansa the way that we live in Europe and to bring him all the gifts he asked for."

Then, and then only, did Henry dispose of his personal rights and properties, one by one.

On August 22, 1460, he formally granted the islands of Terceira and Graciosa to his nephew and adopted son, Prince Fernando, who was King Affonso's younger brother. If Fernando died, the islands would go to his wife, Princess Beatriz, daughter of Henry's own younger brother, Prince João. On September 18, Henry assigned to the Order of Christ all spiritual rights on São Miguel, Santa Maria, Terceira, and Graciosa, and (except for a small amount reserved to pay for masses to be said for his soul) all the income derived from them. On the same day, he transferred any rights he might have in the five known islands of the Cape Verdes Islands to King Affonso. On October 13, he made his will.

He died a month later to the day. Diogo Gomes says he was with him, and he may well have been, for he was at Lagos preparing for his voyage.

"In the year of our Lord 1460," he writes, "the Prince Dom Henry fell ill at his villa on Cape St. Vincent, and he died on Thursday, November 13, in that same year. He was buried in the Church of Santa Maria at Lagos that same night. The king was at Évora at the time, and when word came to him, he and all his people mourned deeply for this so great a man who had won so much in Guinea and who had fought at sea"—that is, whose captains had done this—"such unending battles against the Saracens in the name of our Christian faith.

"Then at year's end, Affonso sent for me, I being still at Lagos paying out what was necessary if the fathers of the church there were to maintain their constant vigils and services in Henry's honor. 'I wish to move his mortal remains to that most beautiful monastery, Santa Maria de Batalha, built by his father, King João. Examine his body and see if I can do so,' he [Affonso] said.

"This I did and found it whole and well preserved except for the bridge of the nose. The body was clad in a rough hair shirt. Well sayeth the Church: 'Thou dost not suffer thy just ones to suffer corruption.'

"The King then commanded his brother, Prince Fernando, and the Duke of Beja, and all the bishops and noblemen of the land to escort the body to that chapel. He would await them there, and the Prince would be placed in the chapel where King João and Queen Philippa and his brothers are buried."

His body is still there—in a beautiful, very ornate sarcophagus, on top of which is his recumbent statue. The navigator is clad in full armor and has a strange, unexplained turban on his head. On the sarcophagus are the arms of the Order of Christ and the Order of the Garter with Henry's own arms. Over it, on a canopy, is a frieze decorated with oak leaves and acorns. It bears Henry's motto: not the newer one, IDA, but the old one: *talent de bien faire.*

But although Henry lay there, his work went on.

He himself described his work modestly. "The Lord has seen fit," he said, "to give me certain knowledge of those parts from beyond Cape Noun to the land of Barbary, and also of three hundred leagues of the coast of Guinea." A mere one thousand miles, he is trying to tell us, of the many thousands he had dreamed of! A mere thirty miles a year!

But, of course, it was much more than that, for it was not the actual lands and miles Henry's captains explored that make him so important to us. It was rather, as his first English biographer, Richard Henry Major, puts it, that he was "the originator of continuous maritime discovery" and sea travel. Systematic maritime thrusting on into the unknown!

For a while after Henry's death, there was a pause in exploration. Affonso the African was too busy with conquests in North Africa to continue Henry's work. But then the ships went forth again. In 1469, Fernão Gomes of Lisbon was allowed to lease all rights to trade with the Guinea coast for five years provided he discovered a hundred leagues a year beginning at Sierra Leone. He lived up to his agreement. Before his contract had expired, his men had not only established La Mina ("the Mine," called this because of the fabulous gold mines nearby) in present-day Ghana, but had gone on to cross the equator. They reached 2° south. In 1482, Diogo Cão (Diogo the Dog) discovered the Congo, and in 1485 he went on to Cape Cross—he called it this because of a stone cross he erected there. Cape Cross is in today's South-West Africa. In 1485, Bartholomeu Dias rounded the Cape of Good Hope. In 1497, as we know, Vasco da Gama reached India.

But India was only the beginning. In the succeeding years, Portuguese captains (sons and grandsons of those whom Henry had trained) went on to Burma, Malacca, what are to-day Cambodia, Laos, and Vietnam, China, and at last Japan. In 1522, Ferdinand Magellan—or rather Magellan's men, for Magellan was slain in the Philippines in a quarrel with the natives—capped all other achievements. They circumnavigated the globe!

But it was not only the Portuguese, however, who fell heir to Henry's aspirations and sought to make them come true by sailing, as a historian of exploration put it, "seas that could not be sailed and navigating unnavigable waters." There were Italians (Christopher Columbus, Amerigo Vespucci, John and Sebastian Cabot—although the two Cabots became Englishmen), Danes (Pining, Pothurst, and Jan Skolp), Dutchmen or men who sailed for the Dutch (Henry Hudson and Abel Tasman), and Englishmen (Sir Francis Drake, John Davis, Martin Frobisher, William Dampier, and Sir James Cook).

In their little ships—Magellan's globe-circling *Victoria* had a tonnage of only eighty-five—they sailed from ports as widely separated as Bristol in England, Texel in the Netherlands, and Palos, Sanlúcar de Barrameda, and Cádiz in Spain. Their object was to explore all the world not yet discovered—from the Northwest Passage, (a hoped-for route to the East which turned out to be ice-choked) to the coral islands of the South Sea (the Pacific Ocean), the spice kingdoms of what today is Indonesia, and the so-called Great South Land, or *Terra In-cognita Australis*, a supposed continent which lay five hundred miles south of Java. This *Terra Australis* turned out to be nonexistent but it gave Australia its name.

Columbus was the most famous of these seafaring explorers. He sailed from Palos on August 3, 1492, and on October 12—only shortly before the twelfth anniversary of Henry's death—landed on San Salvador (Watlings Island) in the Bahamas. Although he did not know it, he had reached the New World, and since from then on travel to this New World was uninterrupted, he is rightly considered its discoverer.

Columbus's voyage was a great feat of seamanship, but even his son agreed that it was Henry who had made it possible.

"It was in Portugal," wrote Ferdinand Columbus, "that the admiral [Columbus had been given the title of Admiral of the Ocean Seas] began to surmise that if the Portuguese could sail so far to the south, he could sail to the west and find new lands."

Maybe it was more than surmise. Columbus's father-in-law was Bartholomeu Perestrello, the first governor of Porto Santo and one of Henry's captains. When Perestrello died, his widow gave Columbus all his papers. Who knows what information he found in them?

Amerigo Vespucci—it was from Amerigo that America got its name—was influenced by Henry too. Henry's advice to his captains was, "If possible, you should *know* before you *do*." An employee of the wealthy Medici family, Amerigo had the money to collect maps, charts, and portolanos. He studied these carefully and became such an expert that in 1492 his employers transferred him to Barcelona and then to Seville. There, as the agent of the Florentine bankers, his principal occupation was the outfitting of ships.

Among the ships he outfitted were those used by Columbus on his second and third voyages, and Amerigo met "the crazy Genoese"—this is what other shipmen called Columbus—who boasted that he had "discovered the islands beyond the Ganges and reached the mainland of Asia."

Amerigo decided to go thither himself and because of his skill as a cosmographer it was easy for him to find a ship that would take him. As ship's cosmographer and navigating officer, he made at least two voyages to the West Indies and South America. On the second of these—it sailed from Lisbon in 1501—he went at least as far south as the Río de la Plata (Buenos Aires is on this river) and may have reached Patagonia.

Unlike Columbus, however, he knew that he had come to a new world, with the result that in 1507 a German scholar proposed that "it be called America after Amerigo, its discoverer."

Pining and Pothurst, who were sent out by the Danish king Christian I to discover new lands in the Arctic, and who actually did reach Greenland and perhaps Labrador, did not study maps or consult portolanos. Instead they took with them a man from the Azores, João de Corte Real, whose father, another João de Corte Real, had been trained by Henry. This João—as the Portuguese proclaim proudly in the legend on a mosaic pavement on the Avenida da Liberdade in Lisbon—was "the real discoverer of America." He and another captain, Avaro Martin Homem, sailed, many Portuguese insist, to *Terra Nova dos Bacalhaus* (Newfoundland of the Codfish) in 1472.

Sir Frances Drake, too, when he sailed into the Pacific on his own round-the-world trip, felt more confident because he had with him a Portuguese pilot, Nuno de Silva, whom he had kidnaped at the Cape Verdes.

So it was with all the others who sailed to explore the seas: directly or indirectly, they inherited the tradition Henry had begun.

But Henry's influence did much more than send seafarers out to sea. As the first patron of scientific navigation, he also encouraged those who stayed ashore to improve the equipment these seafarers used and the conditions under which they lived. This influence, too, lasted long after his death.

Here are three examples.

By Henry's time, men had long since learned how to establish latitude (the number of degrees north or south of the equator). They did this by measuring the height of the sun or of a familiar star and then consulting the tables that every sea captain then had. But longitude (the number of degrees east or west of a determined meridian) was too much for them. They had to use "dead reckoning"—guessing, or measuring with a log, the number of miles the ship had traveled and then correcting this figure for drift, compass course, and other factors. The errors were often great, as witness the distances reported by some of Henry's captains.

In 1729, a Yorkshire landsman, John Harrison, invented the chronometer (a clock which keeps time accurately almost to the second), and now a captain had only to compare the ship's time (which he got by noting when the sun was at its zenith) with home time, which was established by the chronometer. Then he made some calculations and obtained the correct longitude. Oddly enough, this chronometer was first tested on a vessel sailing from London to Lisbon.

In Henry's time too—and for some time afterward—anyone who sailed on a long voyage ran the risk of falling victim to scurvy, and in the mid-eighteenth century, the explorer Sir James Cook decided to do something about it. He noted that those who ate well and kept clean seemed to stay healthy; he therefore saw to it the men on his ships had plenty of fresh meat, fresh fruit, and fresh vegetables instead of the usual "salt horse" and moldy hardtack. He also made them scour the cabins and wash their clothes frequently. He started something, for shortly afterward, every English captain was obliged by law to serve his men lime juice. (Incidentally, that is why the English are now sometimes called limeys.) Cook, in bettering the conditions of his men, was carrying out Henry's traditions.

Finally, in Henry's time, information about currents and winds and weather was very sketchy. But just before the Civil War, an American naval officer, Matthew Fontaine Maury, decided to remedy this. He became an invalid, but instead of retiring, he asked to be assigned to Washington, D.C. There, seated at a desk in the Navy Department, he founded the United States Naval Observatory and the United States Hydrographic Office, which became centers for nautical information of all kinds.

Maury did one thing more—something that Henry in his own way had tried to do. He not only took down from their dusty shelves and studied carefully the forgotten logbooks of every officer who had sailed the seas. He also wrote to every officer (merchant or naval) who still sailed these seas:

"Tell me everything you can about all that you observe and see. About air temperature and water temperature. About wind direction and wind force. About the storms you encounter and the days and belts of calm. About the ocean currents and whether they shift from year to year and month to month or remain constant. Tell me—and tell me in detail."

The information he received he compiled and made available to all seafarers. Because of his work we now have official and accurate "sailing directions" to every part of the world. Henry would have approved thoroughly. Undoubtedly, he would have invited Matthew Fontaine Maury—and John Harrison and Sir James Cook—to his Vila do Infante.

Of course, there were others too. The whole list would fill many pages, and it could be added to yearly if not daily. For oceanography—the study of the sea in all its aspects—is now one of the most important sciences, and ships sail from the United States and Russia and England and France and Japan with equipment (much of it electronic) that Henry—or even Maury—would have envied. With it, they are doing the kind of work whose importance Henry was the first to understand.

So too are the men who navigate the heavens. Just as Henry realized that it was not wise to leave familiar headlands for the open ocean without knowing what you were doing, they understand that men must have knowledge based on careful study and accurate calculations when they seek the moon, the planets, or the stars.

Suggestions for Further Reading

Anderson, Romola and R. C. *The Sailing Ship*. New York: Bonanza Books, 1963.

Armstrong, R., *The Discoverers*. London: Ernest Benn, Ltd., 1968.

Azurara, Gomes Eannes de. *The Chronicle of the Discovery and Conquest of Guinea*. New York: Burt Franklin.

Bradford, Ernle. *A Wind from the North*.

Brochado, Costa et al. *Dom Henrique the Navigator*. Lisbon, 1960.

Cadamosto, Alvise. *The Voyages of Alvise Cadamosto*. London: The Hakluyt Society, 1937.

Camoẽns, Luis de. *The Lusiads*. New York: The Hispanic Society, 1950.

Cary, M. and Warmington, E. H. *The Ancient Explorers*. Baltimore: Penguin Books, 1963.

Collinder, Per. *A History of Marine Navigation*. New York: St. Martin's Press, 1955.

Dos Passos, John. *The Portugal Story*. Garden City, New York: Doubleday & Co., 1969.

Gama, Vasco da. *A Journal of the First Voyage of Vasco da Gama*. New York: Burt Franklin.

Landström, Björn. *The Quest for India*. London: Allen & Unwin, 1964.

Livermore, H. V. *A New History of Portugal*. Cambridge: The Cambridge University Press, 1966.

Major, R. H. *The Life of Prince Henry the Navigator*. London: Frank Cass & Co., 1967.

Oliveira Martins, J. P. *The Golden Age of Prince Henry the Navigator*. New York: E. P. Dutton & Co., 1914.

Penrose, Boies. *Travel and Discovery in the Renaissance*. Cambridge: Harvard University Press, 1952.

Prestage, Edgar. *The Portuguese Pioneers.* London: Adam & Charles Black, 1966.

Sanceau, Elaine. *Henry the Navigator.* London: Hutchinson & Co.

United States Hydrographic Office. *Sailing Directions for the West Coasts of Spain, Portugal, and Northwest Africa and Off-lying Islands.* Washington, D.C., 1952.

INDEX